Low Tide

A Rick and JoJo Adventure

Armand Rosamilia, Tom Duffy

Rymfire Books

Copyright © 2024 by Armand Rosamilia, Tom Duffy

All rights reserved.

No portion of this book may be reproduced in any form without written permission from the publisher or author, except as permitted by U.S. copyright law.

Contents

1. ONE   1
2. TWO   7
3. THREE   13
4. FOUR   19
5. FIVE   25
6. SIX   31
7. SEVEN   37
8. EIGHT   42
9. NINE   48
10. TEN   53
11. ELEVEN   58
12. TWELVE   63
13. THIRTEEN   68
14. FOURTEEN   73
15. FIFTEEN   79
16. SIXTEEN   84

17.	SEVENTEEN	89
18.	EIGHTEEN	94
19.	NINETEEN	99
20.	TWENTY	104
21.	TWENTY-ONE	109
22.	TWENTY-TWO	114
23.	TWENTY-THREE	119
24.	TWENTY-FOUR	124
25.	TWENTY-FIVE	129
26.	TWENTY-SIX	135
27.	TWENTY-SEVEN	140
28.	TWENTY-EIGHT	145
29.	TWENTY-NINE	150
30.	THIRTY	155
31.	THIRTY-ONE	160
32.	THIRTY-TWO	166
33.	THIRTY-THREE	172
34.	THIRTY-FOUR	178
35.	THIRTY-FIVE	183
36.	THIRTY-SIX	188
37.	THIRTY-SEVEN	193
38.	THIRTY-EIGHT	199

39.	THIRTY-NINE	204
40.	FORTY	210
41.	FORTY-ONE	215
42.	FORTY-TWO	220
43.	FORTY-THREE	225
44.	FORTY-FOUR	231
45.	FORTY-FIVE	236
46.	FORTY-SIX	241
47.	FORTY-SEVEN	246
48.	FORTY-EIGHT	251
49.	FORTY-NINE	256
50.	FIFTY	261
	About the Author	267
	About the Author	269

ONE

Ernie Patek looked like a fool, even with the sexy older redhead dangling over him like expensive jewelry.

The obese man was seated at the table right in the middle of the bar, his back to the door but easy enough to spot.

Raul Santiago took his time approaching the couple, heading to the outside bar to watch from a distance. Make sure there was no one else in the bar with the man, heavies seated at another table or wandering on the beach, looking for trouble.

Satisfied after a quick warm beer Ernie was alone, except for the woman, he stood and stretched. That was the sign for his men he was about to enter the establishment and conduct his business.

Punta Prieta was lovely this time of year, although Raul preferred his home in Mexico City to the beaches and scattering of tourists brave enough to travel far from the safe areas of the country.

This was Sinaloa territory, and Raul was part of the cartel here. An agent and a gopher for the bosses, he was only in Punta Prieta because of what the fat man had on his person.

A map, detailing a forgotten shipwreck from a couple of hundred years ago. Hopefully laden with gold and jewels, Ernie had somehow procured it and was in this area trying to quietly find a captain and crew who could help him raise the treasure to the surface.

Word traveled quickly about this fat American buying drinks for the locals and asking his stupid questions.

That word had ultimately gotten to Raul's crew, and he didn't need to wait for an answer from his bosses before he drove out with his men to set a meeting with Ernie Patek.

His initial conversation had been friendly enough, and Raul knew the man wasn't as dumb as he looked. The man hinted at a treasure map, about the levels of security he had in place, about his ties to the CIA and DEA.

Ernie Patek was being backed by the United States government, according to his words and confident smile.

Raul didn't know if Ernie had tacked all of that on in order to seem important and keep from being kidnapped, which would've been easy enough to do.

In fact, Raul had set up this meeting so quickly because he worried any of a number of cartels or local gangs were going to move on Patek at any minute and take the map he supposedly had on him.

The woman would be an annoyance. She clung to Ernie, as if she owned him. By the look on the fat man's face, Raul supposed she did.

"Greetings, friend," Raul said and offered his hand to shake, which Ernie took with a smile.

The woman frowned. This close to her, Raul saw she was older than he'd initially thought. Still very attractive. She might've had some work done: cheekbones, lips, her neck lifted.

Raul knew she was putting those lips to good use with this large man, trying to drain him of every last American dollar he had in his wallet.

Raul knew he needed to get her away from the table and possibly out of the bar itself. He already knew she was his constant eye candy from the reports of his men, so he'd put two of them at the hotel they were staying at. Even if the fat man somehow lived through the next few minutes, and the woman was smart enough to leave the men to talk and went back to her hotel room, they'd take care of her. Shut her up for good.

He doubted she knew anything other than Ernie Patek liked to spend money.

Raul was staring at the woman and didn't sit down across from Ernie.

The woman gave a faint smile and leaned close to Ernie, kissing him on the cheek and giving him an awkward hug. "I'll see you back in the room. Can I order some food?"

"Of course, darling," Ernie said. His attention was on her ass as she left the bar.

"Let's do some business." Raul didn't care about the woman, he was focused on Ernie and what he had on his person right now. If Patek had bodyguards in the bar or outside, Raul knew they were top of the line, because he hadn't spotted them. None of his crew had, either.

"Yes, of course." Ernie turned back and smiled. "She's a wild one. Keeps me awake all night, if you know what I mean."

Raul nodded. "Wife? Mistress? Local whore?" He knew by her few words she was also an American, but Raul wanted to keep Ernie guessing as to his intelligence. An arrogant American in Mexico thought he was smarter than anyone, and would say things he shouldn't be saying. Giving up information because he was better.

"Fellow tourist. East Coast gal. Lots of fun. I think she's separated or divorced from her husband. Came down here for some fun, and she found it," Ernie said and grinned.

Raul knew she was nothing more than a typical gold digger, and wondered how much she knew. "What have you told her about yourself, and the treasure?"

"No, nothing much," Ernie said and put his hands up. "She just thinks I'm a rich man here on vacation."

Raul made a point to look around. "And she never questioned why you're here and not a big city or one of the many resorts?"

Ernie shook his head. "I told her I liked the small, out of the way places. So does she. While she worked on her tan the last few days I put out my feelers to see if anyone was interested in what I had to share."

Share. Raul liked the word, as if this was going to be a joint effort between the cartel and Patek. As if he was going to share in any of the treasure they pulled up. "Show me the map, please."

Ernie shook his head. "First thing's first. Show me the money."

Raul smiled and took out a folded envelope from his front pocket. "All of the banking information is inside. One hundred thousand dollars. Like he agreed upon." The initial payment to Ernie bought into the treasure hunt. A quick look at the map.

Then the work would begin, with Raul promising boats and divers and crewmembers. The treasure would be split evenly, and Raul would get his retainer back in the end.

For Ernie Patek, it was about the excitement. The thrill of the chase. He'd stressed over and over it wasn't about cashing out all the coins and jewelry, but getting his hands on it. No one had seen or touched any of it in hundreds of years.

Ernie took the envelope without looking inside and put it inside the pocket of his thin jacket. Raul guessed to prove this wasn't about the money.

Raul frowned. What was the look that had come over Ernie Patek just now?

"What's wrong?" Raul asked.

Ernie was still digging his hand inside his pocket. He stood, his face red.

Raul stood, wondering what was happening. Was he being set up? He turned to make sure no one was trying to sneak up and intercept him.

"It's... gone. The map is gone," Ernie said over and over, taking off his jacket and patting it down on the table.

Raul grabbed the jacket and checked it himself, hoping the man was trying to play him. He made sure to take the envelope back, even though the money in the account was going to be rerouted out within the hour.

Ernie sat back down on the chair and it gave a groan in protest.

"Where is the woman?" Raul yelled to one of his men near the door.

The man looked scared.

"Find her. She has something of mine," Raul said. He grabbed Ernie by the collar. "You idiot. She robbed you. Us. Now she's going to die."

TWO

Rick lowered the binoculars. The tar on the roof of the building was melting through his sandals. He shifted back and forth, trying to stop the heat from leaving blisters on his soles.

Their plan was going to cause problems, but his heart rate jumped the moment he saw JoJo walk out of the building. There was no turning back. No erasing the avalanche of shit they kicked off.

What were they getting themselves into? The Sinaloa cartel. Some rich asshole with connections to people who lived to cause problems.

Fuck.

It sounded like a good idea when they'd talked about it. But now, realizing what type of power was coming their way, Rick felt a panic attack percolating in his chest.

It was the best idea they had come up with, and it was the worst idea they'd planned. Like they were in a fucking Dickens novel. Hopefully they wouldn't get their heads cut off. And if they did ... well, a chainsaw wouldn't be as quick as a guillotine.

Rick spotted the men who had come in with Raul. He also saw Ernie's men loitering around the area. None of them appeared to recognize the other.

All the better for him and JoJo.

The cartel thought they could sniff out anything. It wasn't just the Sinaloa cartel, but any in Mexico that Rick had been involved with. They all thought they were James Bond, when really they were low-rent, peasant scum who happened to find a way to make money off the lives of the real hard-working Mexicans.

Rick wasn't happy about JoJo putting herself out there again, pretending to hang on to that disgusting tub of lard who flashed his money around everywhere he went. But that was part of the con. Part of any con. You had to shut down the part of your brain that you normally used in social situations. He knew there weren't any feelings between them, but Rick couldn't help but feel jealous watching JoJo with her arms around Ernie, snuggling up to him like a gold-digger.

Rick pocketed the binoculars and headed down the stairs to the first floor and out onto the cracked concrete, burnt by the constant pounding of the equatorial sun. The most important part right now was to help JoJo lose the people who would be following her. The ones who would tail her until she got back to her hotel and then kill her, or worse, before taking back the map she'd pocketed from Ernie. Rick had hoped it would take Ernie a while to notice it was missing, giving JoJo a chance to get out of sight.

By the time he got out the front door of the apartment building, he had to stop to catch his breath. The days when he could chase down a perp over a mile of twists and turns, jumping over fences and dodging traffic, was long behind him. Sometimes Rick felt that he was in better shape when he was shooting horse. Those days were in the rearview, but sometimes he wished for the numbness the drugs gave him, the ability to ignore any aches and pains and keep moving forward, hunting the countless people he had put behind bars.

Most likely it was his diet of tacos, carne asada, anything delicious and fatty that added a couple dozen pounds to his body and got him out of shape. But Rick wasn't giving any of that up, so he preferred to blame his heavy breathing on age and the unbearable heat of the Mexican sun.

Rick turned the corner, walked through an alley, and headed toward the coffee shop they'd planned to meet at.

From the reactions at the bar, Ernie had found out he was missing the map long before Rick thought it would happen. From his dealings with the cartel, running fake passports, he thought there would be more conversation before they got down to brass tacks. They loved to talk. That was the plan he and JoJo came up with in the last couple weeks: get in good with Ernie, wait until the cartel became interested, and then leave Ernie in the dust with no map and no leverage.

But they both thought they would have some more time to get out of the area before Ernie and the Sinaloa realized JoJo had lifted the map.

"Senor Rick."

Rick stopped as he was about to turn the corner and walk into the coffee shop. Nacho, a kid he paid to run paperwork at times, was behind him, standing next to a dumpster that hadn't been emptied since the Spanish had invaded the country.

"Nacho. Hey. I've got some business to deal with. I'll get you the cash later today."

"Ignacio. I told you that's my name. I don't like being called Nacho. That's what gringos eat when they think they're having Mexican food."

"Ok. Listen, I need to meet up with someone. Can we deal with what I owe you in a little while?"

"Senora JoJo is in trouble, si? I saw her leave and a couple people from El Sinaloa followed her."

Rick looked from the alley and toward the light that lit up the main street that cut across it a few feet ahead. He could ignore the kid and keep heading to where he'd planned to meet JoJo, but Rick was shaken from what Nacho had said.

JoJo would know she was being followed. She hadn't survived most of her life navigating the cracks of society without developing a keen sense of her surroundings.

Would that mean she'd still come to the coffee shop? Would she try to lose the men in the maze of the city and contact Rick later?

Ernie didn't know where they lived. JoJo had always been careful to make sure she was never followed back to their bungalow. If she lost the tail, they wouldn't know where to start looking for her.

But Rick knew what Nacho was getting at.

He'd met the kid while Nacho's index and middle fingers were reaching into Rick's back pocket as he was bumped in the street. Anybody else, the kid would have pocketed the wallet and walked off with an apology, the victim none the wiser.

Not with Rick, who'd both caught his fair share of pickpockets, and dabbled in it himself whenever his paycheck hadn't been enough to cover his habit.

"What's your angle, Nacho?" Rick smirked. Besides using the kid as a gopher for random projects, his second favorite thing to do with him was annoy him as much as possible.

"I go to the men following Senora JoJo, distract them so she can get away. You pay me one-hundred-dollars, American."

"What makes you think Senora JoJo can't take care of it herself?"

Nacho shrugged. "Maybe si, maybe no. Do you want to take that chance?"

"And if they decide to just shoot you because you're being an annoying little kid?"

"El Cartel doesn't care about me. I'm what you called me when we met. A, uh, una cosa lives in the water with the spikes."

"A street urchin."

"Si. They don't care about us. Worst case, they throw me across the street, I get a bruise, you owe me another fifty American."

Rick looked over at the alley's exit. He could smell the coffee brewing from where he stood. He'd rather the plan didn't break apart and JoJo met him at the shop. But if she had to start evading the assholes with guns, who knew what would happen. Nacho was right. Rick had seen how the Cartel members handled street kids like him. At best, a shove into the dirt; at worst, a smack across the face and a kick to the ribs.

"Fine. But I don't want to see you at our place until tomorrow, and you better make sure you're not followed."

"Half up front," Nacho said, palm out.

"I'll give you twenty dollars," Rick said, reaching into his pocket. "Two reasons: First, that's all I have on me. Second, that's all I have on me."

He held out the twenty and Nacho snatched it as if a breeze was going to blow it away, up into the sky to be incinerated by the sun.

"Tomorrow," Nacho said, waving the twenty in the air as he hurried to intercept JoJo's tails.

Rick briefly thought that there was something wrong about using a child to distract two grown cartel men with at least one weapon a piece. But the thought was fleeting. There were different rules here, and one of them was not to mess with the street kids. Not out of any kind of moral stance on the cartel's part, but because of the possibility they could grow up to be soldiers.

Rick left the alley, walked into the open-air coffee shop, and ordered a large coffee with cinnamon and agave.

He waited anxiously for JoJo to show up. Not only because he was worried about her safety, but because he had no money to pay for the coffee.

THREE

Raul smiled as soon as the restaurant cleared out. Not even the bartender, waitstaff or owner would dare stand their ground.

The only people remaining in the place were he and Ernie Patek, the fat bastard who'd either set them up or was set up himself. Either way, he was going to pay for his mistake.

"Who is the girl?" Raul asked, looking down the barrel of his gun into Ernie's beady eyes. The man was sweating profusely, and he stunk.

Raul was uncomfortable being this close to the man. He was gross. A typical gringo, who thought his money got him through every door.

The cartel had more pride than that. This American was too stupid to see it, though.

Raul knew his bosses were going to be very pissed off. He worried they'd take it out on him. He needed to figure this all out quickly.

With any luck his men he'd sent after the woman would return with the map and blood on their hands. They knew not to worry about questioning her. They were only interested in the precious map she'd stolen.

The world is full of thieves, Raul thought. "I will ask you one last time... who is the girl?"

"She's... I met her on the beach... she was staying at the hotel... my hotel, you see? I thought she was lonely... I thought..." Ernie began to cry, tears running down his fleshy cheeks.

Raul shook his head. "You thought? No, gringo, you did not think." He chuckled. The man was worthless and not a danger at all. A sniveling coward. Raul pointed the gun at the man's crotch. "You thought with the wrong head. She is very pretty, no?"

Ernie stopped crying long enough to faintly smile and nod his head.

Raul matched the fat man's smile. "It will be my pleasure to slice her pretty face into strips of meat to feed to the dogs on the street, too." He leaned in closer to Ernie, despite the stench. "You will feed all of the dogs in Punta Prieta for weeks."

"No, no, this is not my fault. I had no idea she was a thief," Ernie said.

"You thought she legit liked you then?" Raul was tired of smelling this man. He glanced at the door, where two of his men were standing in the street. "Go and help find her. Do you think I need your help with this *gorda*?" He smiled to himself, using the feminine for fat.

His men left quickly.

"I thought she had some interest in me, and not only my money," Ernie said.

Raul could see the man didn't believe what he was saying. He only got women to be interested because of his flash and money tossed around like it was nothing.

"Where did you get the map?" Raul asked.

Ernie shook his head. "I cannot tell you. I paid a lot of money, not only for the original, but to make sure there were no copies."

"Then I have no real use for you anymore," Raul said. "I was hoping you had a copy. Smart people would've made a copy. Give me your phone."

Ernie took his phone out and handed it over.

Raul sat back down across the table, placing the weapon in front of him. Aimed at Ernie. He began going through the pictures on the phone, hoping the gringo was lying and had taken a photo of it.

No such luck.

"I am truly sorry for you that you weren't smart enough to have some leverage," Raul said. He picked up his weapon off of the table.

"No, no, I can be useful. I can. Trust me. I have memorized the map." Ernie began tapping the side of his head. "It's all in here. Coordinates, islands nearby, everything. You don't need the map. You have me." Ernie licked his lips. "Alive."

Raul wanted so badly to shoot the man in the face. He knew he was lying. This American slob didn't have the intelligence or the patience to memorize the map, but...

Just in case, Raul put his gun away. "Stand up. You'll be going with me. If this is a lie or a trick, the dogs will be fed from your still-alive corpse in the streets. Do you understand what I'm saying?"

Ernie was nodding.

Raul escorted the man out of the cafe and toward his waiting cars.

"You'll be coming with me to the villa, and you're going to take a long shower, because you stink of sweat and fear and tacos," Raul said. "And not the real, Mexican ones. You stink like Taco Bell."

"I like Taco Bell," Ernie said.

"Obviously." Raul pushed the fat man into the back seat of the Land Rover and looked around for his driver. When he didn't spot the man and saw the locals were trying unsuccessfully to not openly stare, he decided to drive himself. His men would figure out how to get back, and hopefully they'd have the map and the woman with them.

"If I got a sketch artist, could you help them to recreate the map?" Raul asked Ernie, glancing at the man in the rearview mirror as he started to drive.

"Yes, yes, of course," Ernie said, nodding his head.

Raul drove out of the town, eyes watching everything. He knew he was also the hunted, and if either a rival cartel, the local police or the DEA got in front of him, it was kill or be killed.

He'd come too far to be stopped now, and the thought of raising a treasure chest of long-lost gold coins made him happy. One of the few things in his life that did these days.

"Where were you born, gringo?" Raul asked, opening all of the windows despite the heat. The fat man was beginning to stink and the stench would seep into the plush seating and could never be cleaned properly.

"Me? Uh, Chicago, but I'm an Army brat. My parents moved around a lot when I was a kid," Ernie said. "I've lived just about everywhere, even overseas for a few years. Italy and Japan."

"How did you get into this particular line of work?" Raul asked, trying to act friendly. Maybe he could still extract some information and wealth from the fat gringo. He definitely had money. Perhaps a ransom was in the future, if Raul was sure there was value and someone on the other side of things, who had access and was willing to part with a chunk of Ernie Patek's wealth.

"I fell into it. An old friend from the year I went to high school in Wisconsin. He exported furniture, family business, and found a way to import and export cocaine, back when it was all the rage. Now, I guess fentanyl and AK-47's are the in thing." Ernie laughed. "He came upon the map when a deal went down badly at the border, right inside Texas. About a year ago."

"What happened?" Raul asked.

"Ahh, you know... the typical double-cross. Can't trust these cartel people," Ernie said. "Um, I mean... no offense."

"No offense taken," Raul lied.

"My friend was wounded. He died a few days later in the hospital. Handed over his entire operation, the legal and illegal, to me, as his only friend. The only person he could trust. He always told me he had something that was priceless in his safe," Ernie said.

"A map? It could be for anything." Raul was getting annoyed. Maybe he should just pull over onto the side of the road and march the gringo into the hills and be done with him.

"No, no, he had paperwork attached to it. He'd done a lot of research. It's from a secret Spanish expedition. Mayan gold. Not only coins but exquisite items, too. No one knows about it.

Never documented." Ernie laughed again. "And I know exactly where it is. Trust me."

Raul certainly did not trust Ernie Patek, and he was going to enjoy shooting the man and leave him for dead, with or without the gold.

FOUR

Most people, when they thought the Cartel, pictured tough, murderous people who could barrel into any town in Mexico and take it over with a bunch of shouting and a spray of an automatic.

They weren't wrong, but didn't know the full picture. American television, as usual, portrayed the Cartel under the exaggerated lights of Hollywood. Sure the Cartel could roll into a town, rain down the fear of God on the townsfolk, and take care of whatever business they were there for. But they didn't know the streets. The alleys blended in with the buildings so you walked by one and never saw it.

If they weren't willing to outright murder someone in the middle of the street, their target wouldn't have too hard of a time getting away, as long as the person knew the streets and its hidden secrets.

JoJo knew every twist and turn in this town, having been here since leaving the U.S. at Rick's invitation. So she should have been able to shake the men following her without much effort.

Currently, though, they were still on her trail and catching up. Whoever these men were, they'd been to town enough times to get to know the layout. This wasn't good for JoJo.

She took a turn down an alley filled with vendors. Despite her better judgment, JoJo took a quick glance behind her. They hadn't rounded the corner yet.

JoJo pulled her shoes off and turned into the next vendor stall.

"Trade?" she asked, pointing to the flip flops on the rack.

The man behind the counter shook his head and pointed at her shoes.

"Used."

"These are Manolo Blahniks. They're worth more than what you make here in a week."

"Three dollars," the man said, pointing at the overpriced sandals.

JoJo rolled her eyes and threw a five dollar bill on the counter. She grabbed the sandals and put them on. It may not be her best idea, but she'd move a lot faster than on heels.

She grabbed a hat on the way out.

"For the extra two bucks."

JoJo pulled her hair up and put the hat on. None of this was the best disguise, but the heels dropped her height an inch or two and the hat hid her long hair. It didn't help that she was wearing a stand-out short one-piece that would be recognized anywhere.

JoJo turned out of the shop, making another quick glance back and recognizing the two men following her about fifty feet back.

She didn't know whether she should meet Rick where they had planned, or stay away from there until she lost her tail. On one end, it would be good to have Rick to help back her up. But on the other end, these guys didn't know who she was and had no idea about Rick. Giving them that extra bit of information may be like giving them an extra hand up in their chase to find her.

Despite the change of shoes and pitiful use of a wide-brimmed hat for a disguise, the form-fitting dress stood out in the bustling alley. Most people chose to wear shorts and sleeveless shirts, or flowing dresses with loose tops.

JoJo could already feel their eyes on her back again.

She turned a left down another alley, then a quick right into a narrower one. She could feel the concrete on each side of her baking from the heat. JoJo avoided the random piles of garbage, probably tossed from the windows of the multi-storied buildings on both sides.

Without having to look behind her, she heard the syncopated footsteps of the two men turn into the skinny walkway. JoJo looked ahead, toward the end where it opened up onto a busy street. The alley appeared to narrow in front of her. The combination of stress, heat, and being following, possibly kidnapped, was getting to her.

The footsteps picked up pace behind her. Pistols racked.

JoJo sped up. She only needed to get to the street and she would–probably–be safe. The Cartel was known to snatch people up in broad daylight, in front of many witnesses. JoJo wasn't sure if she was that important of a risk yet, but then again they most likely wouldn't be following her if they didn't know what she had stashed under her skirt, held snugly in place by a tight garter.

But she had a better chance of slipping away in a crowd then down a garbage-strewn alley with nothing and nobody around.

A half dozen figures came around the corner, blocking the exit to the street. The sun backlit them, making them look like shadows or wraiths.

Or figures of Death that came to block her escape just as she was about to start running.

Small figures of Death. That was odd.

Shouting came from the new arrivals and they raced into the alleys, passing JoJo. She felt a couple hands reach out and grab a thigh or an ass cheek as they went by, but she was too stunned to knock the little bastards down.

What the hell were a bunch of children doing here? Street rats. Street rats who seemed to be crowding the men behind her.

"Señora JoJo, keep moving. We buy you mucho time, right?"

"Nacho?"

"No. Ignacio. Now go."

Nacho raced past her and JoJo hit the street. No point looking behind her. She was well-acquainted with him and his little gang. They'd tried begging for money from her and Rick while two of them attempted to pickpocket them.

They'd almost gotten away with it as well, but Rick flattened one of them against the sidewalk and pulled his tropical shirt back enough to show the butt of his gun. Then he gave them twenty bucks, American, and let them run off.

"What did you do that for?" JoJo had asked.

Rick shrugged. "They seem like good people to have on your side."

Now, as JoJo made her way to the coffee shop, she realized she'd have to apologize for thinking he was a dolt to hand out cash to those rats. Then she realized that she didn't do that.

JoJo made her way to the back of the shop, to the corner table out of sight of the street where Rick sat fidgeting and looking worried. When he saw her, he straightened his shirt and tried to act like everything was cool.

Sometimes JoJo thought he was cute. Other times she wanted to knee him in the nuts.

"Got you a coffee. Agave syrup and coconut milk. Not sure you'd call that a coffee, but whatever. It's iced, which is good since it's been sitting there a while."

JoJo tossed her hat onto an empty table next to theirs and sat.

"Even if it was room temperature, it would still be a blessing in this heat."

"Heard you had a couple of fans following you."

"Nacho told you?"

"Gave him some cash to try to flush the tail off. Looks like it worked."

"Those kids probably have a bigger place than we do, the amount of money you've given them."

"You get what we need?"

JoJo nodded. "Just in time, too. I'd been trying to lift it off him for a while before those Cartel guys showed up. But he was all over me. Even if I had gotten it, I wouldn't have been able to stash it without him feeling it. I really need a shower."

"I could use one myself, sitting here sweating over whether you'd make it here or not."

"You're on. Then I go see You-Know-Who, and we get on this before anyone else does. But first, I'm finishing this coffee. It's delicious."

Rick made a face. "Sugar and cream. Sugar and cream are the only two things that should go in–" He stopped talking as JoJo glared at him.

Rick really wanted that shower.

FIVE

Ernie Patek was sweating. He hoped Raul and his men didn't realize it wasn't just because he was overweight, but because he knew he was in trouble.

He'd lied to the cartel ruffian.

Ernie had glanced at the map a couple of times, but never studied it. What did he care? It wasn't like they made scuba gear big enough for him to go diving around like an idiot.

He had more than enough money to fund a diving team and muscle to watch when they found the treasure and started to bring it to the surface. If the wreck had been in United States waters, like in the Gulf or off the coast of Florida, Ernie would be talking to bad people from his own country and not these Mexican criminals.

In fact, Ernie had tried to involve friends of friends he knew in his hometown, but they wanted nothing to do with it.

"Working within the range of the Mexican cartels, no matter who you think you can pay off, is not a good move if you want to live more than a few minutes of surfacing with a handful of gold coins in hand," his friend told him.

Ernie had finally had to contact the cartel, another friend of a friend, after spending a couple of weeks wasting time attempting to lure an unsavory boat captain or two to dive for him.

No one would do anything without cartel approval.

The meeting with Raul should've gone down without a hitch. If it weren't for the beautiful American woman, right now he'd be getting a suntan with a cold beer in hand, waiting for word of the divers finding the wreck and the treasure.

Ernie knew this was all a huge gamble, and the cartel would just as soon cut him out as the middleman, even though he'd told them he had a buyer in Ohio who would pay top dollar for all of it, no questions asked.

Another lie.

He knew he was way over his head with all of this, but Ernie couldn't help himself. He loved the action and the danger element. As a fat kid growing up, he'd never been part of the group. Never got picked for sports and when he did he was awful. He didn't have many friends, moving around so much, and his mother coddled and fed him twenty four hours a day, seven days a week.

Ernie was her little boy, and until the day she died, she'd done everything for him.

His parent's deaths left him with a nice inheritance, which he used wisely, getting in early on BitCoin and making a fortune.

Some of that money was still making Ernie money as cryptocurrency, and he used it from time to time for illegal activities.

Ernie knew it was all a game to him. He funded meth labs in and around Chicago, not because of profits or even the drugs, but just because... he could. And get away with it, too.

He'd been able to sell microchips for missiles a couple of years back, and knew for a fact they were being used in the Middle East for nefarious attacks. Ernie didn't care about any of it, only the fact he'd been able to do it, and pay off United States government officials to get his product overseas without a second look.

This treasure, though... this was different.

As a boy he'd loved reading about pirates.

Wanted to be one.

Ernie was nine years old when he realized the pirates he'd been reading about were long gone. Decades ago they'd stopped plundering ships and burying their treasure on islands, drinking overflowing mugs of beer with a smiling woman on their knee.

As he got older he found there were newer, better pirates, though, all across the world. Mobsters and cybercriminals and politicians. Taking whatever they wanted, whether they needed it or not, and anyone be damned.

Ernie changed his reading and researching from Blackbeard to Pablo Escobar. He found a love if not necessarily a connection to cartel leaders. The hunger for more and more, and no limit to his greed or the power he would usurp.

He knew the coins at the bottom of the ocean was his ticket to that next level. Hell, to several levels above his current paygrade.

The sky–or in his case, the ocean–had no limit for Ernie Patek.

Raul and the sketch artist were conferring quietly in the living room, Ernie eating plantains in the kitchen. Trying to eavesdrop but failing.

This house was huge, and Raul had said it was nothing. A small shanty he sometimes stayed in, or when he was entertaining local women without his wife or mistresses finding out.

Ernie could see himself in a place like this. Perhaps he'd buy it from Raul when the treasure was found.

"You have the map?" Ernie looked up to see the sketch artist, a thin man with a thin mustache. He was tapping the side of his head. The man looked worried, or maybe it was fear.

"Yes, of course," Ernie said and smiled.

The man turned to Raul and they spoke for a minute in Spanish, or what Ernie figured was Spanish. There wasn't a language called Mexican, was there?

"Tell me where this, uh, thing that is none of my business is," the sketch artist said, sitting down at the kitchen table across from Ernie and opening his satchel. He placed pencils and a large pad in front of him and looked at Raul. "I draw faces, you know? Not maps."

Raul grinned. "I'm sure you'll do a wonderful job, friend. Let's get started. We've already wasted too much time."

The sketch artist pulled out a small dog-eared book of maps and placed it next to his sketch pad. "We can use this as a referral."

Ernie nodded. "Maybe it would be quicker if I looked at the maps of the area and remembered where the treasure was."

At the mention of treasure, Ernie saw the sketch artist shiver. He was definitely scared.

"However you need to do it, gringo," Raul said and sat down between the two men. "I need a map and I need it in the next thirty minutes. Or else."

Ernie took the book of maps in hand and began paging through it, trying and failing not to stall. If he could maybe remember the couple of times he'd actually looked at the map, maybe he'd get lucky.

He knew his life was on the line.

By the look of the man seated across from him, so was his life.

Ernie found a map of the area he was in, nearly absently pointing at a map of the Gulf before realizing his mistake.

A mistake that would've proved costly, Ernie thought.

"I don't need his help, I know where it is," Ernie said and winked at the sketch artist.

I've likely saved his life, Ernie thought. "He can go. I got this."

Raul put up a hand and whistled. Two of his men entered the kitchen, scooped the sketch artist up by his arms and dragged him out of the room.

"He'll be alright... right?" Ernie asked.

Raul shook his head. "No. You said treasure in front of him. He might tell the wrong person. I can't have competition. You understand."

Ernie nodded as if he did. *I am responsible if anything happens to him*, he thought.

"Where is my treasure?" Raul asked, frowning.

Ernie's finger hovered over the map.

He heard the gunshot from outside and slammed his finger onto the Pacific Ocean, right off of the coast. To the left of what might be a small island.

Raul laughed. "Then his death will not be for nothing, right?" He stood and slapped Ernie hard on the back. "As long as the spot you say is right, you can live a long and wonderful life, gringo."

SIX

Alberto Cruze counted the scuba tanks after the afternoon charter left. He'd taken a count of heads when everyone had gotten back into the boat, but you could screw up a headcount. It happened more often than people realized. Since he insisted everybody who chartered his boat use his tanks, a tank count was a guarantee he hadn't left someone in open water. Albert was paranoid about the possibility of losing a customer to the salt water and sharks. But more importantly, he didn't need a lawsuit that took his business and everything else but his short-hairs.

After a quick clean and sweep–tourists could be so dirty–Alberto stepped off the boat onto the dock, taking a moment to regain his land legs. He spent so much time out on the Gulf that he was used to adjusting how he walked to the ebbs and swells of the water. Standing on something solid and unyielding had become foreign to him.

Since he had no more charters scheduled for the day, he headed to the closest bar he could find, which happened to be about 200 feet off the dock. As with most boat docks, there was always alcohol within walking distance.

Not that he didn't sneak the occasional nip while bringing the divers out to the dive site, but he made sure to keep himself somewhat in check while on a charter.

Again, lawsuits.

The bar was open on three sides, the only wall facing the water. Alberto assumed it was there to keep the frequent gusts of wind from blowing the drink napkins and straws all over the place.

It was sparse, with homemade wooden shelves to hold the few bottles of liquor, and a couple of ice chests for the beer. The owner, Mercurio–who everybody called Mercury–was also the only bartender. He never rang anything up on the sand-battered register. Just pocketed the cash and refused to take credit cards, despite the equally battered POS system behind the bar.

Alberto went to the utility sink in the corner and splashed water on his face and arms, washing the dried salt water off his skin.

Mercury had a Modelo waiting for him at his usual spot. Alberto downed half the bottle and sighed. He loved being on the water, but dealing with the annoying customers, no matter how much they paid, drove him to find solace at the bottom of a cold drink.

Alberto looked around the place and then at Mercury.

"Little slow today?" he asked.

The place was empty. Empty and quiet. He could hear the grains of sand moving with the breeze.

"Slow today. Slow every day. You need to tell your charters to stop by here. They just get on their rented Mopeds and drive off to the tiki bars at their hotel."

"You gonna pay me for being your marketing guy?"

"I can't even pay myself. Just figured since you have a three figure bar tab the least you could do is point some rich white folk my way."

"They take one look at this place and hide their money in their shoes. You're stuck with us lowly charter captains, Merc."

"Well, you could at least tip better."

"A dollar a beer. That's standard. Start changing the rules of tipping and the whole world goes to hell."

Alberto was finishing his sixth beer and playing music on his cell phone when Mercury slapped a bar towel in front of him and lifted his chin at something behind Alberto.

He turned to see a tall, long-legged woman heading across the beach toward the bar. He'd known JoJo Mack for years, yet every time he saw her she somehow seemed to get more beautiful. Though she was much older than him, age appeared to be gentle on her.

JoJo walked into the bar, wiping sweat off her forehead, and sat next to him.

"Uno Modelo, por favor, Freddie."

JoJo was the only person allowed to call Mercurio Freddie. He was old school and unfortunately still hung onto a lot of old school thinking, especially when it came to sexual orientation. Being equated with a gay singer of a British band would normally be cause to break a bottle over someone's head. But with JoJo, he was fine. Alberto was almost positive it was because of her charm and magnetism. He had no doubt she'd used it many times in the past to fleece unsuspecting men out of their money.

All Alberto knew for sure was that her and her *novio*, Rick, never came to him unless they needed help with something that was, at best, straddling the fence of legality.

"Heard you've been seen around town with El Gordo," Alberto said, his nickname for Ernie Patek. "I'm not good enough for you?"

"You'll always be my second choice if Rick ever dies. Or disappears. Or whatever else may happen to him."

"You joke, but I'll still hold you to that."

"You can hold me to anything, but it doesn't mean I can't slip away, Allie."

JoJo was also the only one who got away with calling him Allie.

"Got something for you. I can't tell you right now, but it's not safe. That's one of the reasons I've come to you."

"That, and you don't know any other charter captains that will have anything to do with either of you."

"You have a particular way of stating a fact and at the same time throwing an insult in there."

"It's a talent. Lots of practice. What are we talking about here? You know I'm out of the drug running business. At one point I decided I wanted to live."

"Not drugs. Nothing technically illegal, but there will be a lot of heat on us."

"Policia heat, or Cartel?"

"Where one goes, the other follows. You know that. Also whoever Ernie has backing him up."

"Scammed him out of something. I knew it. So you can't give me details, but can you give me an idea of what I get out of it?"

"Enough to stop having to deal with the customers you can't stand. Enough to get rid of that barnacle-covered boat and buy one twice as big that you can live in. Does that work for you?"

"What's on the line? Besides having the Cartel chainsaw my legs off?"

"Sketchy diving, but nothing you can't handle. And possibly chainsaws, but let's not think about that too much. I spent half the day losing a tail before I came here. We're not dealing with geniuses here, but there will be some blood hungry people on our backs."

Alberto looked over at Mercury, who was pretending to wash glasses and not hear anything. Part of owning a dockside bar in the area was the ability to be able to shut your hearing off when it was necessary.

Alberto had dealt with the couple a few times before. There were some tight scrapes, but they always came out on top, and Alberto came out with a few higher numbers in his bank account. Rick had also given him a fake passport for partial payment during one of their past jobs. After being permanently barred from entering the United States, Alberto was now able to travel back and forth without any problems under the name of Jack Reacher.

His only worry was the Cartel. He'd had his run-ins with them when he was moving drugs up and down the coast and they weren't fans of each other. But whatever JoJo had planned seemed to imply that the payoff would be worth the risk. Alberto just needed to know one more thing before he committed.

"Will you be diving also?"

"The three of us, yes."

"You'll have to show up in a bikini to make it look good. Like you're actually paying me to bring you out on the Gulf for some sun and fun."

JoJo leaned toward him and held her beer bottle up to cheers with him.

"I'll be wearing a bikini that will make you salivate more than all the water in this ocean."

Alberto tipped his glass and clinked with hers. There was no need for him to say yes or no. You don't knock glasses together when you're planning on refusing the offer. And they both knew he would do it just to get to see that body in a tiny bikini.

Alberto was no fool.

SEVEN

Baker Cioffi put the binoculars to his face despite the headache pounding in his head. He needed to see if Ernie Patek was still inside and whether he was alive or dead.

He heard the gunshot yesterday and saw the cartel men carrying out a body, but they could easily handle it. Baker knew there was no way it was Patek, unless they'd sliced him up into a dozen chunks. Maybe it would take more.

Baker didn't bother to follow the men when they drove away. He already knew a few dump sites in the area thanks to his intel and the agents that had come before him.

He was alone in this, though. According to his bosses, he was only on vacation, sucking up the sun and drinking in Acapulco.

They knew what he was doing, or guessed they did. He'd been watching Ernie Patek for the past two years and trying to build a case for all of his illegal dealings.

What no one else in the DEA knew was that Baker Cioffi had heard a rumor and now knew it was more than that.

Ernie Patek had his hands on a treasure map, and he was trying to go partners with some really bad people.

Baker had never gone rogue before, not even in light of a few cases he'd worked that could easily be taken advantage of. No, he wasn't going to toss away a career in law enforcement, especially when he had nearly twenty years and a perfect record.

There were rumblings about Baker being promoted to one of the better offices, like Tampa or Poughkeepsie. Instead of being in Milwaukee and freezing most of the year.

He'd earned it because he was an above average agent, and he always did the right thing.

Until now.

Baker wished he had a couple of friends he could trust with this. Even his wife thought he was on assignment in Mexico and not burning vacation time. If she found out she'd think he was having an affair, which made him laugh. He was completely loyal to Suzanne. She was his world, and the reason he was taking this chance.

She'd been diagnosed with cancer. Again. Suzanne didn't want Baker to know, but he could tell. She'd been quiet after her last doctor's visit, and it was easy enough to take a peek in the hospital records and see what she was facing.

Baker wanted to help her, and having the money to get her the best possible help was all that mattered.

Not that he thought he wasn't breaking the law right now, but he knew he could sleep at night.

Baker sat back and closed his eyes. The headache was coming on strong, and the heat and humidity were not helping.

The money wasn't on Ernie still having the map. He knew Raul Santiago had him now, and the cartel wouldn't let Patek walk without first having the treasure in their hands.

Then they'd kill Patek and dump him at the same place where they were going to toss this newest body.

Baker didn't care who was going to get killed as long as it wasn't him. For all he prayed, the cartel could wipe out all of Mexico and every cartel member within a thousand mile range.

These people were animals. He wasn't racist. Baker didn't think these people were human.

There was movement on the balcony when Baker opened his eyes again and he grabbed the binoculars.

It was a very pretty woman, raven-haired with sun-burnt skin. She was wearing a bikini and put a large glass of amber liquid on a table before settling into a lounge chair to get even more sun.

Baker put the binoculars down. He didn't need to stare at another woman, not when he was so in love with his wife. She was either a hanger-on or somehow connected to the cartel.

If she got in the way he'd need to deal with it, but for now his focus was on Ernie and then Raul.

I'm not going to do anything illegal except whatever it takes to get the treasure, whatever it is, Baker thought.

He was a few years from retirement age and he wanted to spend it with Suzanne, not alone. He was sure there were doctors in this world who could cure her once and for all, but you needed to pay for it.

Baker had already spent a lot of their savings to get this far. There was no going back now. Not that their meager savings would be enough to do much for Suzanne anyway. His insurance would be able to cover a lot of the upcoming treatments, but it wouldn't be enough.

He'd need to take out loans and deplete what little they'd saved. Maybe get another mortgage on the house. She'd have to stop working again, and there was no overtime for Baker as a DEA agent.

No, the only way to make this work was to keep tabs on Ernie Patek and grab the man if given the chance.

Nothing stupid, no risk-taking.

Baker had given up drinking and spending too much money on anything. The car he was currently renting was his home for as long as it took. He had boxes of cheap cereal and bottled water he was living off of. No restaurants and no hotel beds.

His friends at work wanted to see all of the great vacation pictures, but he knew he was either going to get the treasure and never see them ever again, or he was going to die trying.

As a last resort, he had a sizable life insurance policy as well as the money he'd get from the DEA if he was killed, which should be enough to pay for Suzanne's treatments.

Baker was rubbing his temples when he saw movement again at the house across the hills.

A black SUV with tinted windows was pulling out of the compound.

He groaned. Should he stay and see if Patek was inside, or trust his gut and follow the vehicle?

Follow. Follow, Baker thought. He watched as the SUV turned onto the main road and headed west.

Baker followed at a safe distance. The cartel drivers would be able to spot a tail quickly, and he hadn't done enough surveillance in his career to feel comfortable trying to go head to head with them.

He was a good distance behind and couldn't see if there were passengers in the SUV or just a driver.

I guess this takes me wherever it takes me, Baker thought. He was doing this all for Suzanne.

EIGHT

All day long men, boys really, in and out of the house. Always making noise, whether from too much tequila and loud music, or power tools biting into flesh. Despite being gagged, whoever the idiot was getting tortured or disposed of could still make noises loud enough to reach any room. They were always idiots. You didn't wind up behind the guarded gates of the property without having done something stupid.

Maria Guerrero poured two fingers of Clase Azul Ultra tequila after Raul left her room. He felt the need to fill her in on every little detail of anything going on in her territory. He could be exhausting, but she guessed it was better to have too much information than too little. Maria was also sure his intentions had more to do with getting an up close look at her. The see-through beach cover-up and bikini outfit–Maria's usual attire–left just enough to the imagination to make most men drool.

Apparently, even though he'd lost the map to some whore, the fat man remembered it so well he could lead Raul and his men straight to the treasure.

Maria knew it was bullshit, but decided to let Raul find that out for himself. The man, although a great soldier, wasted a lot of time on other people's lies. He needed to learn through experience, not by Maria holding his hand.

It wasn't entirely his fault, this inability to read people as well as her. When she'd taken over the territory after her father died peacefully in bed from a heart attack (a rare way to die in this business), her first act had been to kill her father's long-standing Captain.

Maria knew that being a woman was going to cause problems and that the Captain had already been thinking of taking over. She needed to both prove her ruthlessness and get rid of the dissenters at the same time. If not, she wouldn't still be alive.

It helped that Maria was the one who pulled the trigger and didn't just give an order. She also killed two other men who may or may not have been part of a conspiracy to take over after her father's death. Those two were simply to make a point: Maria didn't need a reason to kill, but she needed constant reasons not to.

She'd picked Raul as the next Captain not only because he looked convinced about her ability to run the territory, but there was also something behind his eyes as he watched her execute the men. He looked excited, blood-thirsty, but able to keep those emotions hidden fairly well. Anybody else but Maria would never have picked up on it. That meant he would have no problem taking over and doing what needed to be done day to day, but Raul would also not be a loose cannon, someone to worry about going too far and bringing too much heat.

Maria sipped the tequila and stared at herself in the mirror. She ran a hand through her black hair, revealing a long scar from her temple to her ear. She shuddered as an image from the past flew in and out of her thoughts.

Sometimes, when Maria felt she needed some extra leverage in a situation, she'd tie her hair back, letting the jagged scar show. Even though times had changed, there was still way too much machismo in the culture and in the Cartel especially. Maria had built her reputation over time, but occasionally she used the scar as leverage. An extra push to either get what she wanted or to take someone down a notch in a negotiation.

Everyone in the area she controlled knew the story behind the wound, though most forgot about it until it was right in their face.

Maria could never forget about it, as it was literally written on her face. Also, you never forget anything that has to do with the first person you ever killed.

Maria put her hand down, letting her hair drop and cover the scar.

Before she was interrupted by that unpleasant memory of her past, she'd been thinking about what Raul had told her. About the sketch artist they'd quartered and disposed of yesterday. About Ernie Patek and his insistence that he was some kind of idiot savant and had every detail of the treasure map stored in his head.

Idiot savant. He was half right.

Maria was also thinking about this mystery woman they'd failed to apprehend. That got her fuming and was the main reason she was having a couple glasses of tequila before noon. Raul already assured her that he would have the appropriate measures taken against the two men who let some American bimbo slip away with the map.

Though that wasn't exactly true. Whoever she was, she wasn't a bimbo or a whore. The woman was able to lift the map with ease and evade her men. She was either a talented con given instructions from some as of yet unknown people, or she was working on her own or on the same level with one or two others.

Maria hoped it was the latter. Not simply because it meant less work trying to find out who she was working for, but because Maria loved the idea of another strong woman being involved. Granted, a strong woman she'd have to kill, but was there a better opponent?

An American woman. Someone from the supposedly greatest and most powerful country in the world, here in Mexico trying to take what wasn't hers. Wherever she was hiding, Maria's men would find her.

Maria finished the rest of her drink and refilled the glass, taking another look in the mirror at her hair and what was hidden beneath.

Hiding.

No, this woman wouldn't be hiding. She was no puppy afraid of loud noises and strangers.

Maria grabbed her cell off the nightstand.

"Raul, take a couple of men and go to the docks. Whoever this woman is and whoever she's with, they're going to be looking to charter a boat." Maria listened to Raul's stupid question. Maybe she'd been wrong putting him in charge. "Because she's American. Most likely whoever she's with is also American. I doubt they took their own boat down here. They'll need to hire someone. Also, ask around about any boat captain that's been involved in anything other than taking tourists' money."

Raul asked about Ernie Patek.

"Leave him here. He has no chance of getting off this property. Let him wander around and sweat all over the place. I don't care. I'd rather him be here than out in public where he might have a slim chance of escaping."

Maria hung up and sat on the edge of her bed.

They'd definitely need someone to help navigate to the treasure. Maybe even help collect it. That's how she'd find this woman. Not scouring the streets, but sniffing out whoever the unlucky person is that she chooses to hire.

The sound of the garage door opened jolted Maria out of her thoughts. She listened as the car drove down the driveway and the gates opened and closed.

Maria tossed her cover-up off and walked out to the balcony. She needed a nap, and between the buzz from the tequila and the sun tanning her already bronze body, she'd probably be able to get one in. A rarity for her.

Maria spotted the glint of glass in the distance and immediately ignored it. She'd long ago learned not to react to anything unusual. She never wore hats, but if she did she wouldn't tip it.

She laid down on her lounge chair and closed her eyes.

An idiot with binoculars spying on the compound for some reason. A spy who didn't know well enough to buy binoculars with lenses that didn't reflect the sun.

It wasn't the police or the government. While she didn't have everyone in her pocket, she had enough that she would have gotten a message if either of the two were trying another failed attempt to take her down.

That only left one logical conclusion. Another American in their midst. From which three-letter alphabet agency, who knew?

A car started up in the distance and moved in the same direction Raul had gone. Maria played with the idea of phoning him and telling him he had a tail, but he'd find out soon enough. And if this person knew so little as to give himself away without even making a noise, then he'd soon be in their hands.

Then, Maria would extract whatever information she wanted. Extracting by extraction.

NINE

Rick stared at the needle and sighed.

Outside the hotel window, he could hear laughter as children kicked around a makeshift soccer ball of old socks taped together. He'd promised Nacho he'd buy a couple of real soccer balls for the street urchins, but was afraid to use his Amazon account.

Of course, he could easily take a walk down to one of the many markets and purchase a couple for a few pesos.

He'd need to add it to his list, but right now he was struggling with the needle and its contents.

Rick had been clean for many months. He never came close to slipping again, to falling down the spiral of drugs and his addiction.

Yet... here he was. Again.

He'd been watching the dealers from the hotel window for the last few days, knowing exactly what was happening. Rick had gotten the itch again, and he didn't know how to scratch it without shooting up.

If JoJo even thinks I'm doing this again, she'll kill me, Rick thought.

He knew they had a really good thing going, not only between them but with the things they were accomplishing. This treasure score could set them up for life, although it meant getting out of Mexico and spending the rest of their lives in splendor on a continent not part of the Americas.

Rick glanced at the needle on the small table again.

His mind was arguing back and forth, like the stupid devil and angel on your shoulders bullshit.

One fix isn't going to hurt. It will reset and make you better.
One fix could kill you. No cue what's even in that needle.
One fix is the problem and the solution so often.

Rick went back to looking out the window. JoJo should be back soon, and hopefully she'll have a ship and a captain to help with the salvaging.

He'd told her he was Scuba certified, which was a lie. He'd done it a few times for fun, but it had been half a lifetime ago. He'd also been in much better shape, too.

With any luck, Rick wouldn't have to get in the water. He could stand on the deck with a beer in hand, helping the crew to pull up vast amounts of gold and silver and whatever else was down there.

Then they'd have to worry about the crew either turning on them or telling the cartel where to find us. This was all so very risky, and Rick knew they were walking a tightrope.

With so much on the line and so much wealth, Rick knew he'd need to shoot his way out once they got the treasure. This was not going to end well for JoJo, either.

Rick hoped they survived this.

JoJo should've been back by now. He stared up and down the street, knowing she'd slip in through the side door and not be seen.

There were too many people outside, and Rick knew most of them would be spying for the cartel. They'd be seated with their eyes half-closed, watching and waiting. Information was key in this and most Mexican towns, and the word had definitely gotten out there was an American female that had something the cartel wanted.

Any information about JoJo could set a person and their family up for life.

Rick popped his head back inside before someone noticed him. Not that he thought he was a person of interest yet. The longer he could keep himself anonymous the better, though.

Back to the needle.

He could be very happy in a few seconds if he picked it up. Forget the stress of life for a few hours.

And start this wild ride again, where nothing is more important and JoJo finally has had enough and leaves, Rick thought.

He closed his eyes and sighed again. Rick had finally gotten the drinking under control, kind of, but he knew all of that would be tossed with one prick of the needle.

Rick often wondered how his FBI career would've gone if he wasn't an addict. Would he still be on the job, helping to spread democracy and freedom for America? He didn't believe any of that rubbish, but knew he'd be in a good place right now. Solid paycheck, a team underneath him, and lots of hot women.

But all of that was long gone.

It was down to Rick and the needle. Yet again.

Someone yelled down on the street, breaking Rick's concentration and dark thoughts.

He looked but whatever had happened was already gone, moving along in the flow of daily life.

The kids were still kicking the sock ball around. Lots of men and women moving, going through their boring lives.

Rick saw two men carrying automatic rifles duck into the cafe across the street. They could be here to kill Rick and JoJo, but more than likely to force the owner to pay protection money for the cartel.

Life in Mexico was fun and dangerous.

Rick knew if he got high he'd be in trouble. JoJo would know immediately and be so mad.

But maybe the high was worth it.

Rick panicked when he heard the key in the door.

He grabbed the needle and tried to hide it in the small area between the window screen and the ledge, but it slipped from his hand.

Down below, onto the street.

Groaning, Rick nearly dove out from the third floor after it.

"Hey, what's up?" It was JoJo.

"Nothing, I uh…" Rick shut the blinds and sat down on the bed. "How'd it go?"

"Very well… I think." JoJo grabbed her sweatpants and a t-shirt. "Put the air on. It's too hot."

"Broken again," Rick said and shrugged. "I went downstairs and told them."

And then I went outside and bought a needle filled with death, Rick thought. *Or absolute pleasure*.

"I'm going to get changed out of these clothes. Maybe take another shower, if the water is even working," JoJo said and went into the bathroom.

Rick didn't move until he heard the water running before opening the blinds and looking down at the street.

The needle was gone and no one was looking up at him, all engrossed in their own lives.

Rick wondered if he dodged a bullet.

He wondered how many more bullets he'd need to dodge before one caught him right between the eyes.

TEN

Besides Rick, there was only one other person in the world JoJo trusted to both keep a secret and have her back. And lately, the way Rick had been acting, he may have gone down a rung on the trust ladder.

JoJo put it down to nerves. After all, who wouldn't be a bit shaky when the eyes of the cartel were searching for them? Rick was never the coolest of people when it came to any job that had to do with cash. Forged passports? He was like Rico Suave. Possible violence, loss of limbs, death? He was like Woody Allen on speed.

For now, nervousness was what her brain was using to rationalize his change of mood lately. JoJo didn't want to even think about the other possibility.

After her shower, she picked out an appropriate baseball cap, a pair of beachcomber glasses, and a ratty t-shirt and jeans. There was nothing she could do about her height, but hopefully dressing the opposite as the alter ego the cartel was looking for would keep her under the radar enough to do what she had to do.

Rick was still sitting by the window, looking pensive. She gave him a kiss and squeezed his forearm, just below the crook of his elbow and watched to see if he flinched. As much as she didn't want to think he would slip back into his addiction, she needed to be certain. What they were about to do required mental clarity and focus.

"Give me an hour. If I don't phone by then, you know where I'm going to be," JoJo said.

"I still don't understand why I can't go meet him. The cartel, Patek's men, know nothing about me."

"Because he hates you and you'll wind up with a glass of whiskey thrown in your face."

"I got him into this country. Don't know why he's still such an asshole."

"Because he thinks of me as a daughter and he knows your background. He's over-protective, but that's a good thing. I'd say not to worry, that he'll come around eventually, but that probably won't happen. He's a stubborn old bastard."

"And you care about him."

"I care about you, don't I? What's the difference?"

JoJo gave Rick another kiss and left the relative safety of their hotel to meet with the other person she trusted her life with.

Professor Apollo Gatanis sat at the outdoor eatery, brushing crumbs off his khaki, button-up shirt. His Panama hat was tilted forward to block most of the sun's rays, though with his already weathered face, The extra UV wouldn't have made much of a difference.

As JoJo approached, she smirked. He looked like he should be in Cuba having a Daiquiri with Hemingway. All he was missing was the cigar.

They'd snuck him out of the States a few years ago, bringing him over with one of Rick's passports. To the townsfolk, and the country of Mexico, he was known as Jeffrey Hanneman. But JoJo would always think of him as Apollo, or Apo when she was trying to be endearing.

JoJo wasn't one-hundred-percent sure what he'd done to have to leave the U.S., but his mumblings when he was a few whiskeys into the day had something to do with the university he'd worked at–and where JoJo had been his student–and misappropriation of funds.

Being a history teacher, whatever funding was mishandled couldn't have been that much. JoJo couldn't imagine there were a lot of grants and stuff like that going to a subject about things that had already happened.

Apollo saw her coming and stood up to give her a hug, pieces of tortilla chips tumbling off his shirt and onto the sidewalk.

"Josephine, it's so good to see you. You don't come visit me as much as you should. I'm old and lonely and have nothing to do but eat and drink, read and sleep."

"That sounds perfect to me, Apo. I probably stay away because you're the last person on earth who calls me Josephine." They both sat and JoJo ordered an iced coffee and two carne asada tacos. Dressed as she was, she didn't care if she stained her shirt with the delicious salsa and hot sauce.

Apollo finished his whiskey, the ice clinking against his teeth, and gestured for the waiter to bring another one.

"What number is that on this bright, early day?"

"It's number none-of-your-concern. I'm retired and in a tropical paradise ... sort of. I can do what I want."

The waiter brought out another drink, along with a plate of two massive burritos smothered in cheese and pico de gallo.

"Apparently what you want is an early heart attack."

Apollo dismissed her comment with a wave. "So tell me. Do you have it?"

"No, not on me." JoJo gave him the rundown of the map and the basic location, along with what Ernie Patek had told her was down at the bottom of the ocean.

Apollo nodded, slurping from his glass, and leaned back.

"Manila galleons." Apollo noticed the confused look on JoJo's face and continued. "Spanish trading ships that sailed from the Philippines to the west coast of Mexico from about the sixteenth to the nineteenth century. They carried many things, including precious artifacts and gold from China. Gold coins? Possible. But either way, from the underwater LiDAR description of the wreck, this is a Manila galleon. No doubt."

"Is it worth the effort? The trouble?"

"The danger, as well? Depends on how much you trust this information. Sounds like the man you got it from isn't too trustworthy. Then again, none of us are. Otherwise, we wouldn't be sitting here under assumed names, enjoying our banishment from our home country.

"Obviously any silk or spices will be long gone. You may find some porcelain, but who gives a loud shit about that. You'll find a good amount of Chinese artifacts that will be worth a lot, but a pain in the ass to fence. Coins are your best bet. Melt them. Shape them into bars. Anyone will buy it, no questions asked."

"Can you help with the other stuff? The harder items to get rid of? I know your connections in this field. That's why we're sitting here."

"Those items belong in a museum!" Apollo slammed his fist on the table, turning the few heads that sat at the other tables.

He laughed. A deep, guttural laugh that came from the depths of his belly and exploded from his mouth like an erupting volcano.

"Indiana Jones. What a twat. Those items belong in the hands of whoever will pay the most." Apollo leaned back again and sipped his whiskey, staring at the people walking past.

JoJo knew that look. It was one he got back when he was teaching her in class. He'd just suddenly go off into his head for a moment, wheels spinning. Then he'd come out with something brilliant about whatever the subject for that day's class was.

JoJo waited.

Apollo's eyes came back into focus. He turned to her and smiled, then burped awful whiskey and burrito breath into her face.

"I can help you. For a cut, obviously. But I need something from you."

"Whatever you need, Apo."

"I need you to get Ernie Patek out from the cartel."

ELEVEN

Ernie Patek knew he was in so much trouble and would likely be killed like the sketch artist, but he couldn't help himself.

He was leaning against the wall with one hand while the other one took care of himself, the curtains pulled back an inch so he could stare at the woman in the bikini on the balcony nearby.

She was absolutely gorgeous, and when she rolled over onto her stomach and took her time adjusting her position, with her great ass in the air, Ernie sped up.

She was looking at her phone and he saw her lips moving as she read. He imagined those lips wrapped around…

"When you're done doing that, feel free to come out and talk to me, fat American pig," the woman yelled, moving her sunglasses up and staring directly at where Ernie was self-serving.

Ernie stopped and ducked away from the window.

"Come outside. I'm not asking you," she said.

Ernie composed himself, getting his shorts and shirt just right, before opening the glass door and stepping outside. "Lovely day, huh? Nice and sunny."

He made sure not to stare at her, looking out over the nearby homes and to the ocean.

"Sit and tell me a few things about yourself," the woman said.

Ernie grabbed a chair from a nearby table set and made sure not to block her sun and not to be so obvious and stare at her. He angled the chair so he wasn't facing her, as if the ocean was more beautiful. "What do you want to know? My name is Ernie. Ernie Patek. Is Raul your boyfriend or something?"

She laughed. "What do you want to drink? Tequila? Lame American beer?"

"Um… got any bourbon?" Ernie smiled. Maybe they'd get drunk together and have some afternoon delight. It would be cool on so many levels. Besides her being so damn hot, Ernie would have something secret over Raul, who he was not a fan of.

She reached under her lounge chair and rang a small bell.

These cartel people are so lazy, Ernie thought. He was hoping she'd get up and get him a drink, serve him, and he'd be able to see those hips in motion.

A small woman appeared, her eyes downcast. "Yes, ma'am?"

"Two bourbons. Some cheese and sausages, too."

The small woman nodded and rushed off.

"Ernie Patek," the woman said, sitting up and taking off her sunglasses. "What brings you to my home?"

"Your home? It is very nice, senorita."

The woman shook her head. "Maria Guerrero. I detest formalities. In my home, in my world, we use first names. Even nicknames. But never full names. It is part of the business we do, you understand."

"I do," Ernie lied. He felt like he was always behind when it came to talking to these people. They said so many words and confused him.

"Raul is not my boyfriend," Maria said and shook her head. "He works for me. You see, Ernie, I am the leader here. Not only in this part of Mexico but for a large chunk of Sinaloa. There have been some changes at the top, and I ended up on top."

"Oh, uh… congratulations." Ernie's smile dropped but he regained it. If what she was saying was true, she was the boss of the cartel. Which meant he had a chance to bang the boss. If he played his card's right.

"You brought something I wanted but then you lost it. Why?" Maria held up her hand when the small woman returned with a tray filled with various cheeses, crackers, meats and vegetables, along with an unopened bottle of bourbon and two whiskey glasses. She set it all down, with a generous pour of the bourbon, before leaving.

"Why?" Maria repeated.

"Why did I lose it? That wasn't my fault, not really." Ernie picked up the closest glass of bourbon. "I mean, technically it was, but I had no idea that woman was going to steal it."

"Everyone is a thief," Maria said. "Did you tell Raul everything you knew about this woman?"

"Yes, of course." Ernie was nervous and he downed half of the bourbon before building a cracker with cheese and sausage.

Maria sat up, not touching any of the food or drink. "Now, tell me what you didn't tell Raul. I need to hear it from you, Ernie."

"Nothing. Seriously, he knows it all," Ernie said, shoving the food in his mouth.

"And you still know where all of the treasure is, huh?" Maria tapped the side of her head and smiled.

Ernie was staring at her plump red lips. He'd give anything to kiss her. "Uh... yes. It's all in there."

"What if I said I didn't believe you? I could have you tossed off of the balcony," Maria said. "You wouldn't die but it would likely break your legs and you'd be left to cry like a bitch until you finally died or an animal ripped you apart. Would you like that?"

"No, of course not. I am telling you the truth. I know where the treasure is. I already told Raul." Ernie finished the rest of his bourbon but didn't know if Maria was going to pour him another glass or let him do the honors.

"And when they realize you've lied, and we waste a lot of manpower and resources, and the woman who stole from you has the treasure in her hands? Then what?" Maria was staring at Ernie, who had to look away.

"I'm telling the truth," Ernie lied.

"Let us all hope so, because I'd hate to have to kill you slowly. Maybe tossing you off of the balcony would be too good for you," Maria said. "I'll string you up in the center of town and let the locals deal with you as a warning not to cross me and my cartel."

"You do what needs to be done, ma'am." Ernie glanced at the bottle of bourbon.

Maria smiled. "Please, help yourself. Finish the bottle and my glass. I'm not thirsty. The food is also yours." She stood, grabbing a folded towel and wrapping it around her body in one deft motion.

"Thank you, ma'am."

"Maria."

Ernie smiled and grabbed the bottle. "Maria. Sorry."

She leaned forward and Ernie couldn't pull his eyes from her ample bosom.

"If I catch you pleasuring yourself while watching me again, I will have your tiny American pecker removed and shoved down your throat, to be washed down with bourbon. Do we understand one another?" Maria didn't wait for an answer as she left the balcony.

Ernie sighed. He was in deep trouble.

He sucked down her glass of bourbon and refilled both glasses. If he were going to die shortly, he might as well enjoy some food and drink.

At some point soon he knew they'd know he was lying and his life would end.

TWELVE

The town wasn't a big tourist trap with half a dozen all-inclusive resorts and buffets with food tamed down for the American palette. It wasn't insular, though. There was a decent sized population of Expats, mainly from America, but a handful from Europe.

Alberto was lucky enough to snatch up most of the actual tourists. Enough to stay in business. Which was fine with him. The other ones, the ones who lived in town and around the outskirts, tended to be people running away from something.

Most of them kept to themselves. The last thing they wanted to do was a boat tour or go diving in with sharks.

Rick and JoJo were the exception. Alberto was sure they were running from something or someone, but either the threat had passed, or they were deluding themselves into thinking they were safe. The two of them wandered around town and on the beach like a celebrity couple.

Alberto had helped them out a few times, with some little things. He never asked. If it was any of his business they would have told him. Besides, the less he knew, the less the information could be beaten out of him by the cartel, or some American gangster tracking them down.

This new plan he got himself roped into, though–whatever it is, it sounded like there would be heat all over anyone involved. And it was already too hot in Mexico.

As if the sea gods had read his mind, a black SUV pulled into the gravel parking lot. Alberto didn't need to look to know the group stepping out of that car.

"You're supposed to protect me, not send these bitches my way," Alberto mumbled to lapping waves as he finished tying up the boat.

Another car pulled in shortly after, but parked further down the lot. Obviously a rental. Obviously a gringo.

Based on the loud shirt Alberto could see from that far of a distance, possibly DEA or ATF. He'd seen undercover agents plenty of times before. They all dressed like they thought they were slick and being touristy. They were all wrong.

Alberto had enough time to get out of sight, but ultimately that would be pointless. They'd see his boat and want to talk to him. Raul and his men obviously weren't here for a joyride.

He watched as they sauntered over to the dock. At one point Raul glanced behind him at the man in the car, but turned away quickly. Whoever that guy is, he just got himself into a world of trouble.

"'Berto. How's the fishing business?" Raul asked, taking off his glasses.

Alberto didn't flinch at his stare as so many others did. They'd grown up together, ran the streets as kids just like that little Ignacio and his bunch. Alberto wasn't stupid enough to think that their past gave him any protection if he pissed off Raul, but he certainly wasn't afraid of him.

"Scuba, Raul. Lots of money to be made from the tourists, right?"

"Scuba. Fishing. Same difference. Throw those Americans in the water and see who gets eaten."

Alberto shook his head and began rolling up the extra boating line.

"Only sharks around here eating people are you guys."

"You could have been a shark, too. Instead you chose to be a guppie." Raul lit a cigarette and walked to the edge of the dock before backing away a little too fast.

Alberto smirked. Raul never was comfortable off of dry land.

"Speaking about making money, have any good deals come in recently? Someone wanting to charter your boat. Maybe offering a little more than usual?"

"I wish. Been thinking about raising my prices anyway. Slip rental keeps going up and filling the tank on this boat costs about as much as those shoes you're getting sand in. What's this about, Raul? You know I'm not involved in anything anymore. My business is clean."

Raul dropped his cigarette into the sand and stomped it out. He gestured for his men to take a walk.

"We go back a long way, amigo. That's why I know, even though you say you've gone straight, something comes up that seems like a good deal you may slide a little off the straight and narrow. Not like you haven't done it before."

Tires crunched on gravel and they both turned. Raul's men had been approaching the guy in the car, who was now pulling out of the parking lot a little faster than someone with nothing to hide should.

"Should we follow him?" one of the men asked.

"And leave me here with no way home?" Raul asked. "Just let him go. Whoever the idiot is, he'll be back."

"Are we done here?" Alberto asked. "Because I need a beer and, no offense, I'd rather enjoy one without your company."

"We are done for now. But listen to me, 'Berto. This is not something you want to be involved in, because it will be the last charter you ever do. And that's just me being the messenger. Everyone involved will wind up at the bottom of the ocean."

"Well, then it's a good thing I have no idea what you're talking about. I get someone trying to book me for something that seems strange, I'll let you know."

"I'm sure you will," Raul said, his eyes showing that he didn't believe it.

Raul held out his hand and Alberto took it. It was coarse and the grip strong. He could feel the scars on Raul's knuckles from where they used to punch cinder blocks hanging from an exposed alley beam. They both were trying to toughen up for the future. To become what Raul achieved and what Alberto turned away from.

He never told Raul why. He never would.

Alberto watched them leave, heading in the opposite direction as the NARC. Probably going to the next set of boat slips to interrogate the captains. Alberto was sure that they wouldn't get as easy and relaxed a visit as he did.

But just because Raul had approached him with the air of an old friend didn't make him one. The cartel was your friend only if they needed something. The moment you weren't useful, you were dead to them. Most often literally instead of figuratively.

Alberto would need to get a hold of JoJo, and be careful about it. Raul would have someone watching him. JoJo came to him not only because they had known each other well, but because she knew he was probably the best person for the job. If she knew that, then Raul knew that.

She'd been clear there would be heat on this, but Alberto didn't think it would start so soon. He didn't even know what she and Rick had planned.

Alberto was walking to the bar when he saw the car with the undercover agent come into view. He shook his head. The guy really needed to learn how to be inconspicuous.

Instead of going past the docks and following in the direction of Raul, the car pulled back into the parking lot. Except this time he parked in the first spot, closest to the beach, the boats, and Alberto.

Alberto stopped mid-step.

The man got out of the car and straightened his ugly tropical shirt. Then, he lifted a hand at Alberto and headed his way.

Great, Alberto thought.

THIRTEEN

"Baker is a strange first name," Alberto said to the man seated across from him. He knew this was risky, out in the open, but he'd already told Raul he was going to get a beer. Besides, the DEA agent was buying at least this round. He'd hear him out, drink the free beer and tell Raul what was said the next time he saw his old friend.

The cartel was always looking for more information and Mexico was crawling with DEA, CIA and the rest of the American alphabet soup groups trying to shut down the cartels.

Alberto smiled at the DEA agent again.

"It's a family name, Baker," the man said. "That's not important."

"Ahh, but it is. That's where you're wrong, Baker. Family is everything out here, you know? I make a decent living not because of gringos wanting a boat ride, but because of standing in the community. Because I was born and raised on these streets. Not more than three blocks from where we sit was the house I became a man in. True story. My allegiance is to the people of this town and to Mexico."

Baker Cioffi shrugged. "What about money? What about living a better life in another place, where your skills could be properly used? Where you could become something important and bigger than you could ever be here?"

Alberto grinned, showing off his two missing teeth. "The United States is no heroic place for a man like me. I am fine right here, doing what I'm doing. You need me way more than I'll ever need you, so I'm not sure why you're even bothering with me."

He was trying not to be obvious, but Alberto was worried Raul or one of his men would spot him chatting with this DEA fool. There were too many eyes on the street, too many on the payroll of the cartel.

Alberto finished his beer and slid the empty toward Baker, wondering if the man would buy him another round.

Baker smiled and waved a hand at the bartender, holding up two fingers. Alberto noticed the man hadn't taken more than a sip of his own beer.

"Got time for another beer and a few more questions?" Baker asked.

"Have you asked any questions?"

Baker gave a faint smile. "There's something happening in town, and I figured you of all people would know what it was."

Alberto waited until his beer was brought and took a sip before answering. "So... is this an official fact-finding mission of the DEA, or do you actually know something is happening?"

"We know there is something big happening, and we want to stop it or get involved."

Ahh. There it is. Getting involved meant the United States government wanted this treasure for themselves, keeping it for their own gain, all the while waving their flag and telling the world they saved the poor Mexicans from the evil cartel again, Alberto thought.

Baker leaned forward across the table. "We're willing to pay you handsomely for any information leading to our end goals, if you catch my meaning."

"I'd like to see the paperwork for this, then," Alberto said, as much to annoy the gringo as to back up a bit and give himself some time to think. He knew working with the DEA was a death sentence… if anyone caught him.

While Alberto enjoyed his life in town, he knew this wasn't going to end well. Old age was never a sure bet, especially when you worked around the cartel. One false move and you disappeared without a trace, and no one was stupid enough to come looking for you. No, Alberto knew he needed a backup plan.

More than one if possible.

"I can get you this all in writing," Baker said. "We can start with a handshake agreement."

Alberto put a hand up. "Don't even try it. Someone sees me shaking your gringo hand and I'll be dead before nightfall. Can I trust you, Baker?"

"Of course. You have my word. I want to stop this before the cartel gets richer," Baker said.

Alberto smiled. "Richer? Is this about money, then? I'm still not sure what you're ultimately after, you see? I'll need more information before I can shake your hand."

Baker sat back and tapped the side of his beer, still not drinking it.

"I think you already know why I'm here," Baker finally said.

Alberto shrugged and couldn't help but grin. "I have my suspicions but I need to hear everything you know, or this won't be happening. What is the lame American expression again? Ahh, yes... hard pass."

Baker looked like he was about to push away from the table and leave, which would've been fine with Alberto, too. He already felt overwhelmed between working with JoJo and having Raul at his back. Adding the DEA to the mix might be too risky, but in the end the reward might be worth it.

"There's sunken treasure," Baker whispered, looking around. "We think there's a man who has a map of the location, and we think the cartel has him. That means the cartel will hire a captain to take them to the location and pull up the gold."

Alberto smiled. "Gold, you say? Are you sure?"

"As sure as we can be. What else would be down there, right? Likely a Spanish vessel overflowing with gold items from some Mayan raid." Baker took a sip of his beer. "Anything is possible, but it has to be something of value for the cartel to go through the trouble of kidnapping a man for it."

Alberto shrugged. "Could also be nothing more than a rumor. If every time someone mentioned a sunken ship filled with treasure off the coast of Mexico or The United States... surely, more would have been found by now, right? It seems like we're all still little boys chasing a pirate's treasure."

He obviously hoped the treasure was real, but he knew better than to admit it to the DEA agent. Better to play dumb for as long as possible. Even if he had three potential bosses in this, three different angles, he'd need to play this as far as he could and see which of the three ended up with the treasure.

Alberto hoped it would be him in the end.

"Then you'll help us?" Baker asked.

Alberto laughed. "I'm not sure which of my words you took to mean I was throwing my lot in with the DEA. Surely–"

Baker stood. "I suppose you already know you have no choice. I'll be in touch. If the cartel is asking for your service, I'd take them up on it. What's the old saying, huh? Keep your friends close but your enemies closer."

Alberto shrugged. "Great movie and great line from it."

"I'll be around," Baker said and left the bar.

Alberto finished his beer and realized the damn gringo had never paid the tab, leaving him to do it.

FOURTEEN

Grace had taken it too far this time. Nathan heaved some more chunks of his lunch over the side of the boat, wondering why he'd been stupid enough to eat right before getting on her father's yacht, and why he'd agreed to go out into the water to begin with. It's not like he didn't know he'd be throwing up until his sides hurt.

He had a distant cousin in Florida, a cop, or an ex-cop or something, that couldn't get on the water either. Seasickness ran in the family.

But Nathan knew why he'd agreed to go out into the choppy Pacific waters: Grace had a monthly stipend larger than an entire year's worth of his salary, she was smoking hot, and it's what she wanted to do. What Grace wanted, Grace got.

Probably been that way since she was born, Nathan thought as he dry-heaved.

Nathan wasn't too bad on the Gulf where, if not placid, it was at least a lot calmer than the Pacific. On the Gulf he could usually keep his food in his stomach. This up and down, side-to-side sharp swells was some bullshit.

They'd anchored way out of sight of land, though the ocean wasn't as deep as Nathan thought it would be this far out. The anchor hit bottom at one-hundred and twenty feet.

He'd heard of sudden drop-offs. Where you'd be a few dozen feet deep, then suddenly an underwater cliff would drop the floor a thousand feet. Nathan had seen it on something Grace called a depth-finder. Before the rocking got to him, he was almost mesmerized watching the numbers go up and down.

Nathan stayed bent over the side of the boat, waiting for another surge of nausea, while at the same time hoping a giant shark would pop out of the water and bite his head off. End his misery.

He read the lettering on the boat, even though he was looking at it upside-down, because he'd seen it too many times: So What?

Nathan thought the name was strange at first, until he got to know Grace and her family better. He realized people swimming in that kind of dough didn't give a shit about anything.

Right now, Nathan wanted to re-christen the boat Hell No!

Grace stirred from where she'd been working on her tan at the bow of the boat. Nathan heard ice clinking, then rattling, then a groan of frustration.

"Get it yourself, I'm sick here," Nathan yelled across the thirty feet between them.

"I can't, Nate. If I move I'm gonna ruin the evenness of my tan."

"You're just going to spray tan over it in a week. Who cares?" Nathan paused a moment before smiling at his brilliant thought. "So what?" he called over to her.

"Shut the fuck up about the boat's name for once and get me a drink." There were a few seconds of silence. "Or, I guess I can put my top back on and do it myself."

Nathan spat into the water and wiped his mouth. She knew how to manipulate him, even in the middle of him being sick. What Grace wanted, Grace got.

"Can we please get out of here?" Nathan asked, handing Grace a refill. He cringed at how whiny his voice sounded.

"Come on, Nate. We're supposed to be on vacation. Do you know how many guys would kill to be on this amazing boat with this amazing body?"

"I know we're on vacation, and I promise you we can do all the vacation things that don't involve water. All on me. We'll go shopping. We'll lay on the beach. Go to a museum." Grace gave Nathan a look. "Ok, forget the museums. Whatever you want, I'm willing to do it. Just … not this."

"Willing to do it with my money," Grace mumbled into her glass as she took a sip. Nathan decided to ignore the comment. He didn't want to get into an argument out on the water while his stomach was still churning. Also, she wasn't wrong.

Grace put the drink down and laid back. It took a few moments before she realized Nathan was standing in the way of the sun. She looked up at him and sighed.

"Fine. But I want a romantic dinner at that restaurant we saw, and then sex."

Grace wasn't interested in having sex but knew it would shut Nathan up and he would only be able to focus on that.

"Remember how I showed you to lower the anchor? Do that, but the opposite."

"Ok, Captain. Oh, regarding that restaurant–"

"I'll pay for it. I'll just let Daddy know it was you so he doesn't think you're even more of a loser."

"I'm not a loser."

"I know, baby. But Daddy doesn't. Now raise the anchor and let's go."

The chain started coming up but stopped after a few feet. The entire contraption shuddered and he heard Grace curse. She ran over and stopped it.

"Fuck. We're stuck on something."

"Well, what if you drop it, move the boat a bit and then we try to raise it again?"

"That's stupid. I'll just dive down and see what it's caught on."

"How are you going to dive down that far? You don't even have a suit or anything. I'm pretty sure that's some sort of expert level diving."

"The water's pretty clear. I have a portable tank, so I can probably get far enough down to get an idea of what we're stuck on."

"And how is knowing what the anchor is stuck on going to help us fix it when you can't dive down that far?"

"Daddy will come or send someone. But aren't you interested in finding out?"

"Why would I be? Probably some underwater cable or something, like in that *Jaws* movie where they raise it up and make Jaws bite it."

Grace covered her ears. "Spoiler alert, douchebag."

"It was like, one hundred years ago. Anyway, your dad didn't seem too happy when we all flew here to begin with. What makes you think he's going to be gung ho to come rescue us."

"First, because I'm his daughter. Second … well, all that matters is I'm his daughter. He might leave you for the sharks, though."

Grace grabbed the small oxygen tank and dove in the water. Her head popped up and she flicked her hair back. As much of a pain in the ass as she could be, it was moments like this–her wet body glistening in the sun–that reminded him of why he stayed with her.

"What are you never supposed to say in a horror movie?" Grace asked. "I'll be back."

She went under and put the mouthpiece in. Nathan watched bubbles rise to the surface as she purged the water. He didn't know why, but this new situation of being stuck out in the middle of the ocean seemed to have calmed his upset stomach. It must be the distraction. Also, he wasn't looking forward to having to have her father come and rescue them.

A little while later, Grace's head broke the surface. She tore the mouthpiece away.

"Call my dad."

"What? What happened?"

"Call my fucking dad. The anchor's attached to a piece of wood."

"Ok, and?"

"The piece of wood is attached to a giant wreck of a ship." Grace climbed back onto the boat. "This must be why."

"Why what?"

"He had these coordinates saved on the GPS. He must have been meaning to come here."

"You're saying your dad came down here to look for a shipwreck?"

"How do you think he makes his money, Nate? Mopping up at Walmart?"

She reached into his pocket and took his cell phone.

"What's he under in your contacts?"

"Uh, his name. I mean, I can call him it's …" Nathan watched helplessly as Grace looked up her dad's contact.

"Ernie Fat Fuck? Really, Nathan?"

Nathan shrugged and started thinking about how he would clear this one up later.

"Who is this?" Grace asked when the phone connected. "It doesn't matter who I am, you Mexican whore. Put my father on the phone now. Excuse me? Are you Mexican? Are you with my father? Then you're a Mexican whore. Now put him on. Finally. Thanks bitch."

Whatever Grace wanted, Grace got.

FIFTEEN

"Speakerphone, Ernie," Maria Guerrero said as she handed the fat man his phone. She glanced at one of her men near the doorway, who was holding an assault rifle in hand, waiting for Ernie to follow her gaze and nod.

"Hey, honey... how's it going?" Ernie asked.

The man was sweaty and smelled so bad. Maria would force him to take a shower, a long and hot one, as soon as this phone call was done. She'd also ask about his daughter, because she was going to have her men kidnap the little bitch and torture her for a few hours.

"Daddy, me and Nathan–"

"Nathan and I, dear," Ernie said. "Let's not be commoners like Nathan."

His daughter groaned on the other end of the line. "Please stop saying things like that. I like him. We're having fun. While you do whatever it you're doing with that Mexican skank whore at the hotel, I'm enjoying myself. Taking in the sights of Mexico. I haven't been down here since graduation weekend. Remember that? Probably not, because you were all coked up and hitting on my friend's moms at the airport."

Maria waved her hand to hurry the call up. Not that she thought Ernie was going to say he'd been kidnapped. His ego was too big to admit it, especially to his daughter. He'd act like he was in charge.

She shook her head. How did a man this disgusting have offspring? He'd had money for a long time. That's the only thing that made sense.

"What's the matter, dear? Daddy is quite busy right now."

"Yeah, with your Mexican slut. I get it. Anyway... the anchor is stuck," his daughter said.

"On what?"

"A shipwreck." His daughter sounded so excited. "There were coordinates in your yacht that took me here. I dropped anchor, Nathan and I were getting some sun. Well, I was, he was getting sick. Nearly puked on the deck but I told him to do that off the side or you'd kill him."

Maria sat down across from Ernie and smiled. Now she was interested in the conversation. A shipwreck? Coordinates? While Raul was spinning his wheels with a supposed map, Ernie knew exactly where the treasure was this entire time.

He was definitely smarter than he looked.

"I never programmed any coordinates into the yacht, honey. I don't actually do anything more than relax and enjoy the view," Ernie said. He wiped sweat from his pudgy face. "I don't know what you're talking about."

"Well, I know I didn't do it. Anyway, I dove down but it's like over a hundred feet deep, but I can definitely see it. The water is so nice and clear," his daughter said.

"Stay out of the water. There are sharks in the water." Ernie smiled faintly at Maria.

"Yeah, Nathan already ruined the ending to that *Jaws* movie for me. Jerk."

Maria put a hand over the phone and grinned. "Tell her to give you the exact coordinates and we'll go and help you to get the anchor off of the shipwreck."

Ernie shook his head. His hands were shaking. "I think she needs to do it herself. This is a teachable moment. Do you have children, ma'am? This is how they learn."

Maria shook her head. She was no longer smiling. "Tell her to sit tight. We'll be there soon. You and your Mexican whore."

Ernie had fear in his eyes. He knew what was happening. His daughter had said too much.

"Say it," Maria said. She took her hand away from the phone.

"Sit tight, hun. Daddy will be there very soon. Don't leave that spot. Got it? See you soon." Ernie disconnected the call. Maria took the phone back.

"You've been lying to us," Maria said as she stood, shaking her head. She leaned against the couch and took off her stiletto shoes. "These are killing me feet."

Ernie had his hands up. "No, I didn't lie to you. I swear. I have no idea where she is right now, but there's no way it's at the shipwreck. I don't even know where it is. I promise."

Maria sighed. "Which is the lie then, Patek? That you don't know about the map's exact coordinates, or you don't know about the yacht coordinates?"

"Both. That's what I'm telling you. I don't want to die," Ernie said.

Maria looked at his phone. "We can follow your daughter through the phone."

"Please don't hurt her. She didn't do anything wrong," Ernie said.

"She called me a Mexican whore. I'm Colombian, to be fair. I wonder how pretty she is, and if she'll still be pretty once I'm done with her," Maria said. "And it sounds like you're not a big fan of her boyfriend."

"No, I am not. He's using her for her money. For *my* money. Nathan is a snake."

"Then it will give me great pleasure to have Nathan torture you for a few hours. Let him get out all that aggression he likely has for his girlfriend's annoying and controlling father," Maria said. "Get up. Time to take a cruise."

She pointed at the guard in the room. "Don't let this fat bastard out of your sight. We're heading to the docks. I want six men with us, too."

"And Raul?" The man grabbed Ernie roughly by the arm.

"Is Raul in command, or am I?"

"You, ma'am."

"If I want to involve Raul I'll do so. Until then… it would be wise for you to do as you're told. Understood?"

The man bowed low before dragging Ernie out of the room.

If Maria could get to the yacht and secure it, she could have some fun onboard while she found skilled divers within the cartel to assist in the recovery of the treasure.

The look on Raul's face when he returns and sees she'd done all of the hard work, while he drives around town chasing phantoms, Maria thought. It would be another nail in his coffin.

Maria intended to pound as many nails into it as she could, so there'd be nothing left for Raul in the end. He was a parasite, a virus she needed to be rid of. He was a liability to what she was hoping to accomplish.

She knew if Raul obtained the treasure, he'd use it against her. He might try to buy favors within the cartel from it. He might try to wrest control, too. Mara knew Raul didn't take too kindly to a female in charge. He was too old school, he'd been raised by his arrogant father and grandfather.

Maria checked Ernie's phone, making sure it was charged enough so she could find his daughter and watch the little arrogant bitch plead for her miserable life.

SIXTEEN

Rick sat under the Ahuehuete tree, halfway up the hill that led down to the dirt road across from the boat slips and the weather-worn, white-washed bar owned by Freddie Mercury, or whatever his name was.

The tree offered some shade from the sun, but was slightly disturbing. Rick felt like he was sitting under a giant, furry spider, ready to drop down on him and suck his blood out until he was just a husk of a human.

Nacho sat next to him, pulling dead grass from the ground and tossing it into the air. The slight breeze from the ocean pushed the pieces behind them.

Rick had been enjoying some alone time with JoJo when the kid had knocked on their door. Then, after the knocking was ignored, the pounding started. Rick opened the door, grabbed Nacho by the collar and slid him up the side of the doorframe.

After Nacho used his bare feet to rip the towel off Rick's body, forcing Rick to drop the kid and cover himself up, Nacho explained why he was there.

And now here he was, under this weird spider tree, spying on the one person JoJo had vouched for. Not that it took too much convincing for Rick. He'd spent plenty of time with Alberto through the years, running up and down the coast for various hand-offs and payments.

"Why are you shaking, Senor Rick?" Nacho asked.

Rick looked down at his hands and quickly folded his arms across his chest. Shit, he hadn't even shot up, hadn't smoked, hadn't snorted anything, yet his body was already acting like it needed a fix.

"This tree freaks me out. Just tell me again what you saw."

"After we rescued the beautiful Senora JoJo from the two men, I sent two of my own men to follow them. We knew where they were going anyway. Back to that compound they always go to. I told them to wait down the road on their scooters and follow any car that leaves."

"Two of your men? How old are they? Thirteen?"

"Older than you in experience, and bigger cojones too."

"Watch it, Nacho."

"Ignacio."

"Whatever. Finish the story."

"I told you already. They came here. They talked to the boat man–"

"Alberto."

"Yes, I know his name. He's the boat man. Then they shook hands and left."

"And this guy with him now?"

"No clue who he is, but look at how he's dressed. Obviously from your part of the world, Senor–"

"Just call me Rick, please. Every time you add an extra word to your already long explanations it makes me want to go to sleep."

Rick didn't have to ask. He just wanted to know how on the ball Nacho was. Rick knew the posture, the mannerisms, the way of dressing, from back in his days being a Fed. Plying information out of suspects with drinks was another known tactic.

Rick looked over at Nacho. He had another handful of burnt grass in his hand and let it fly behind him with the breeze.

"What are you doing?" Rick asked.

"Testing the wind."

"For what?"

"In case I need to play the golf or shoot someone with an arrow."

Rick stared at the kid for a while before standing up.

"You're a special kind of stupid, aren't you?"

"I'm special. You're stupid. Hey, if we team up, that could be our code names."

"In your dreams, Nacho." Rick headed down the hill.

"Where are you going?" Nacho called out.

"Need to have a talk with Alberto now that the Fed is leaving. You still have eyes on Raul?"

"I have eyes everywhere, amigo."

"Good. Keep them there."

Alberto was finishing his beer when Rick sat next to him. Alberto looked up and sighed.

"What did you and your girl get me into? First I get the cartel coming to say hello, then some American Federale bastard who stiffed me for the drinks."

"What did you tell them?"

"Nothing. What the hell could I tell them? The little I know wouldn't give them shit."

"It would put me and JoJo on their radar."

"You two are already on their radar. You're on the whole country's radar as far as I know."

"But they don't know who we are. Not yet. They find out you're taking two Americans out? They'll beat our names out of you."

Alberto finished his drink and grabbed one of the warm ones the Fed hadn't touched.

"You give me too much credit. They wouldn't have to beat me too much. And if you're so worried, maybe you shouldn't be sitting here right now."

Rick grabbed the other warm beer, took a slug, and immediately regretted it. The only thing worse than warm beer was warm beer in hot climates.

"They know what JoJo looks like, not me. I'm an unknown at the moment. What about the Fed? What did he want?"

"Same shit they always want: to get their hands on whatever your bounty is. Of course, they say they want to take down all the bad guys and blah, blah, blah. They want money just like the rest of us."

"Do you think he's going to hassle you again?"

"Does a fish shit in the ocean?"

Rick opened his mouth and closed it. Did fish shit? He wasn't sure. Didn't really care. But the question threw him off-balance.

"Everybody poops," Alberto said, seeing the confusion on Rick's face. "Didn't you read that book?"

Rick pushed the beer toward Alberto and stood up. He dropped a twenty on the table.

"Do me a favor. When the Fed comes back, chat him up a bit. Get some more info on him."

"His name's Baker, and he's with the DEA."

"That's a good start, but I mean more than that. Like why he was sent down. What he's really here for. Something doesn't make sense to me. Why would the DEA send an agent here for a lost trea–" Rick cut himself off, but it was a little too late. He saw Alberto's eyes light up.

"Another six beers and I didn't hear that last part," Alberto said.

Rick threw another twenty on the table.

"Just dig into him. I'll try to get some info from a couple people in The States."

"And if Raul comes back asking more questions?"

"Don't worry about Raul. I have him covered at the moment."

Rick left the bar and walked over the hill to where his bike was parked. Nacho was gone. Rick hadn't expected him to hang around. The kid seemed to be everywhere at once, his hands in everything. Rick just hoped trusting a gang of teens and pre-teens to keep an eye on the cartel was a smart move.

It didn't sound smart when he thought about it.

SEVENTEEN

Nathan was getting on her nerves again. He kept pacing the deck and whining about being trapped in this yacht, as if it were a bad thing.

"My father will be here soon," Grace said. "Get me another tequila. Get yourself one, too, so you lighten up and stop being so annoying."

At first she thought he wasn't going to do it, but Nathan sighed and went to the bar. He might be a dolt. He might not be a great lover anymore, now that he was getting fatter and more comfortable around her, but he had his uses.

Like a lap dog at this point, Grace thought.

"Why did you put ice in my tequila? Did I ask for ice?" Grace groaned, about to either toss the glass overboard or in Nathan's face, when she saw a speck on the horizon. She smiled. "Here comes my daddy to the rescue."

"Finally," Nathan said and glanced at his Panerai Luminor Marina watch, which Grace had bought for him. Nearly nine thousand dollars, all so she could have a boyfriend wearing an expensive watch when he took her out in public.

I'll have to get the watch and the other things back when I eventually grow tired of him and break it off, Grace thought. She knew it was coming sooner than later, too. Nathan was starting to bore her with all of his negative talk and worry about losing his job because he was never actually working. *Maybe I'll let him get fired first and then break up with him.*

The approaching boat was much smaller than one Grace thought her father would be caught on, and as it rolled up smoothly to the side of the yacht she saw why.

It wasn't her father at all.

Six armed men hopped onto the yacht. Nathan screamed like a girl and dropped his tequila.

Grace smiled when Cuba Zayas, the boat captain who worked for her father, climbed aboard the yacht. "Took you long enough."

Cuba looked confused. He was an older man with deep, brown eyes. Long flowing curly hair and an amazing tan from being on the water so much.

Grace knew his friendship with her father went back even before she was born. She trusted the man, and knew he would do good for her family. She'd also had a crush on him since she was twelve years old.

"Time to go," Cuba said. He was smiling at Grace.

"Why all the guns, huh? Afraid Nathan would finally man up and say something?" Grace laughed at her joke. She knew Cuba and her father both disliked effeminate Nathan. He wasn't manly like they were. At least Cuba was. Her father, it was rumored, used to be skinny and tough back in the old days. Before she was born.

"Why are you in this spot?" Cuba asked, glancing at Nathan. "Go fetch me a bottle of whatever the lady is drinking. Now."

Nathan ran off and Cuba sat down across from Grace. "I asked you a question."

Grace shrugged. "I saw the location in the yacht and decided to see what it was. Nothing but clear blue skies and water. But the anchor got stuck on a shipwreck below."

"You've seen the shipwreck?" Cuba asked. "You dove down to it?"

"Not all the way. I went down far enough to see what it was. Why? How do you know about a wreck?" Grace asked.

"Who do you think programmed the ship to come out here? I was about to get a team together when you took the yacht, so I changed my plans and followed you," Cuba said. "Not that I thought you knew what you were doing, but when you came to this very spot, the spot I was planning on diving at some point... you see how it looks fishy?"

Grace shrugged and took a sip of her tequila. "Just out here getting some sun. Not even sure what you're talking about."

"No, of course not. Your father would never tell you about his dealings. Why we're in Mexico right now. Why he's been so busy with meetings, when this is supposed to be a vacation for all of us." Cuba shook his head. He took the bottle of tequila from Nathan when the man approached, topping off Grace's glass. "I suppose it is a smart move to not let you in on the family business, on the secrets. Safer for you. Besides, all you care about is you and him." Cuba glanced at Nathan again.

Grace smiled at Nathan. "He's okay. Getting boring, though. I might need a change."

Cuba stood quickly and had a Glock in his head, aimed at Nathan's head. "Change is a good thing."

"I'm kidding," Grace said and chuckled. She got off on seeing how scared Nathan was right now. How macho Cuba was being in front of her, too. It was a huge turn-on. "Or am I?"

Cuba pulled the trigger and shot Nathan right between the eyes.

Nathan slowly fell backward, a look of terror still on his face.

"He pissed himself like a child," Cuba said, pointing at the wet pants of Nathan. "What kind of man is he? Was he?"

Grace put her glass down before she dropped it. Her mind was still trying to process what had just happened, so suddenly and so out of the blue.

"Come with us. We need to torch the yacht to cover the shipwreck," Cuba said. He motioned with his hand for Grace to get up but she was paralyzed.

"Get up, bitch. So sick of you and your rich girl shit," Cuba said and yanked her up by the arm. "Take her to the other boat." He took her cell phone and tossed it overboard.

Grace was led to the other boat, where she was put into a seat overlooking the yacht.

Cuba and his men began moving throughout the boat. Grace had no idea what they were doing until she saw the smoke from below deck.

"Here," Cuba said as he got onto the other boat with Grace. He handed her the bottle of tequila and a clean glass. "I think you'll need this."

She poured herself a glass, filling it to the top.

The yacht was aflame now.

By the time they got two hundred yards away, the yacht was sinking.

"Hopefully it will land just right and cover the shipwreck, so we can come back in a few days, once we have the right equipment, and take the treasure," Cuba said.

"Is that why my father is down here?" Grace asked.

Cuba smiled. "Yes. He's figured out there is a vast treasure down below. He thought he could pay us all peanuts to help him and the cartel extract it. As if the damn cartel wasn't going to kill us all as soon as it was onboard."

"My father trusted you with the location and you're backstabbing him," Grace said.

Cuba shook his head. "No. He didn't. I was nothing to him, as always. He thought of me as beneath him. I was muscle and nothing more. Never an equal partner."

"So now what? Why did you kill Nathan? Why did you save me?" Grace asked.

"Nathan was annoying. I knew if we kidnapped both of you, he'd get on my last nerve. To make my life easier, he went down with the ship."

"Kidnapped? Wait... you kidnapped me?" Grace took a gulp of her tequila. This was even worse than she thought.

EIGHTEEN

At first, Maria Guerrero was confused. She saw nothing but water and sky. There was no yacht, no Ernie Patek's daughter. Nothing out of the ordinary.

"Are you sure this is where she should be?" Maria was going to be very upset if Ernie had played her in some way.

"Yes, yes." Ernie was staring at his phone. This was definitely the last place her phone pinged from. One of the men who works for me made sure to have all of our phones tied together via satellite. I watch my daughter as much as possible. She's a bit... wild. Her boyfriend, Nathan, is also a gold-digger and I'm trying to pry them apart, but so far Grace is digging in her heels and saying–"

"I don't care about your stupid daughter and her boyfriend," Maria said. "Where is she?"

Ernie shook his head. "The signal died half an hour ago but it was set to this coordinate. Maybe she's... oh, no. No, no."

Maria watched as the fat man went to the side of the ship and peered down into the water. "Is she dead, maybe? Maybe the yacht ran aground on a reef or something?"

If I toss him over, will it really matter? He is so useless to me right now, Maria thought. Yet, she knew that wasn't entirely true. He had information she needed. As long as there was any chance, no matter how small, he could help her, Ernie was going to be kept alive.

"Then this is a dead end and we're exposed out here," Maria said. "Bring us back to port." Then she had an idea. "Better yet… head to my villa at Rosarito. We can begin everything there."

"No, my daughter might be down there," Ernie said, waving his fleshy hands. "We have to send a diver down."

"If she's down there then she's dead," Maria said. "Likely she got the anchor freed and she's on to her next adventure." She took his phone back. "I'll be monitoring it, in the event she reappears. Maybe she turned it off because she felt foolish for getting her daddy involved. Maybe her boyfriend and her are doing the nasty and didn't want to be disturbed."

"He needs to keep his hands off of her," Ernie said.

Maria laughed. "Ahh, such a proud papa. My father gave me to one of his associates when I was twelve, as a business transaction."

"That's awful." Ernie shook his head. "Wow."

Maria smiled. "It toughened me up. I knew there was only one person I could trust. Me. It started me on this path and I thanked him every day he was alive, until I'd finally had enough and smothered his cancerous face with a pillow several years ago. It was a good thing, all of it."

Ernie was frowning. He legitimately looked upset for her, which made her laugh. Men were so weak.

"I'm going to ask you one more time, Ernie Patek… do you actually know where the treasure is or not? I'm getting sick of wasting time with you."

"Yes, I know where it is," Ernie said, obviously a lie.

"I'm going to give you twelve hours to get your story straight and tell me where we're headed," Maria said. That would give her enough time to figure out what she was going to do about Raul and his men loyal to him, too. She had no delusion Raul would play nicely with her, especially with so much at stake.

He'd either wait until the treasure was found and then try for a coup, or had a plan in motion to take her out beforehand, making it look like a rival cartel or the Americans, and then immediately finding the treasure and looking like the hero.

Maria didn't know if Ernie's daughter was going to be a missing piece, either. It would've been nice to have her as collateral so Ernie wouldn't try to do something foolish.

She turned to Ernie. "Who drives the yacht, normally? Obviously your daughter or her worthless boyfriend knows how..."

"No. Nathan is not allowed to touch my yacht. Grace knows better," Ernie said.

"So, did you or Grace sail down the coast to Mexico?"

Ernie sighed. "I have a captain. A loyal friend who works for me. He did."

"And where is he now?" Maria was trying to be as casual as she could be, letting Ernie keep talking and giving her the information.

Ernie shrugged. "He said he was going to be around, but I don't keep tabs on him."

Maria smiled and held up his phone. "I thought you kept tabs on everyone in your circle, right?"

"Oh, yeah, I suppose so," Ernie said. "Cuba Zayas. We've known each other for many years. Always a good guy. Got me out of a few scrapes in the past."

"A partner?" Maria asked.

"No. Just a friend who I can rely on."

"Why not a partner?" Maria sensed there was something more to this story. If she found someone loyal who could be trusted and she'd known for many years, who had helped her to move up the ladder... she would definitely give that person the proper titles and kudos. Ernie seemed to want to push this person away, if she was reading between the lines.

"Long story," Ernie said.

Maria smiled. "We have several hours until we arrive. Tell me about Cuba Zayas."

"He, uh... well, I'm not sure I want to tell you this, but... well..."

"Quit stalling and talk." Maria turned to one of the men nearby. "I need a drink. Surprise me."

"He slept with my wife many years ago. They never told me but I knew. I don't know how long the affair went on, but he betrayed me." Ernie shook his head. "A part of me never forgave him. Or her, for that matter. I keep him close because he does some amazing work for me. Always has. That never stopped."

"So, despite the man not being loyal to you, he's allowed to live and be around you because he makes you money?" Maria asked.

"Yes, he makes me and my family a lot of money. He's amassed an impressive amount of contacts over the years, and his ability to buy his way through any trouble we might encounter is legendary," Ernie said. "Enough to make me look the other way with the personal things."

"Aren't you worried about your daughter around him?" Maria asked and then grinned. She could see by the look on Ernie's face she'd struck another nerve. "Wait... Grace is his daughter, yes?"

Ernie wiped tears from his eyes and bowed his head.

Maria almost felt sorry for the fat man, who'd been cuckolded by someone he trusted. She hoped Ernie had manned up and killed his wife, too.

She doubted it, though. He didn't seem like he had the cojones to do it.

NINETEEN

While Rick was out doing whatever it was he did, JoJo sat on the creaking wooden chair, her feet up on the table, smoking a cigarette. A habit she long ago had given up, but recently acquired again. It was her little secret, and an easy one to keep.

Rick had broken his nose so many times, his sense of smell was almost non-existent. Unless he walked in and caught her in the act, he'd have no idea. Still, JoJo made sure to brush her teeth and spray a little perfume on her neck afterwards.

The other thing, more concerning to JoJo, was that Rick had seemed distracted lately. Sure, he paid enough attention to her in all the ways that mattered. But in any downtime they had, she caught him being lost in his head, fidgeting with something or running his fingers up and down his forearm.

JoJo knew the mannerisms well.

Rick wasn't using again, she knew that much. JoJo would be able to tell. But he was thinking about it. And, worse, he was trying to hide his thoughts from her. Instead of sitting her down and communicating, like any people in a healthy relationship should, he told her he was just stressed about money, or the next job, or some other bullshit.

JoJo snorted and dropped her cigarette into the mug of water she used as a makeshift ashtray.

Healthy relationship. Is living on the lam, putting each other in danger, a healthy relationship? JoJo thought.

Of course not. But it was a hell of a lot of fun.

JoJo stared at the sealed envelope on the table. They hadn't opened the stolen map yet. There wasn't really a point until they had the basics lined up. Mainly the diving equipment and the right captain for the job. JoJo vouched for Alberto, but Rick wanted to make sure, always the more careful of the two.

Besides, she'd had to listen to Ernie drone on and on about it that she already knew most of the specifics: a dive close to the limit of most licensed divers; shark-infested waters; and no guarantee that the treasure would be just sitting there at the bottom waiting for someone to lift it out of the water. There was a good chance it could be buried under a large amount of silt and sand.

It wouldn't be easy. Considering the depth and the amount of time it could take to find it, unbury it, and bring it up, it would take multiple dives. The depth would also require them to stop at multiple intervals for a considerable period of time while surfacing to let the nitrogen clear their bodies.

The last thing JoJo wanted to do was spend any amount of time in a hyperbaric chamber. Or worse, spend the rest of time being dead. Though, considering who she stole the map from and who had chased her through the streets, death was certainly on the table.

She'd gotten into plenty of close calls in the past, but this might be the most dangerous.

Her phone buzzed on the table, one of a hundred burner phones she'd had since coming to Mexico.

It was good for calls and that's it. No texting. No internet. No Caller ID.

JoJo didn't need to know who was calling. Only one person knew the number.

"How'd it go," she asked, and lit another cigarette. If Rick was calling, it meant he'd be back soon. Might as well get another cancer stick in.

"Cartel are all over Alberto. But we figured that would be the case. Didn't factor in the DEA, though. I fucking love surprises."

JoJo heard Rick's heavy breathing. He must be on his bicycle. When did he get so out of shape?

"Why would the DEA have anything to do with this? We're not digging up kilos of cocaine."

"Trying to figure that out. I have ... goddamn how long is this hill? ... I have Nacho and his little midgets keeping tabs. Damn kid seems glued to my hip lately."

"More like glued to your wallet. You did check you still have that, right?"

"He's a good kid. Besides, he already had a couple of his buddies tailing the cartel. We wouldn't have found out about the DEA guy if it wasn't for him."

"What about Alberto?"

"He kept his mouth shut. Not that he knows much of anything. Said the DEA wants to use him as an informant, but didn't seem to really give specifics about what they were after. I think the guy was fishing. Maybe saw Raul and his men talking to Alberto and figured he'd try to pry some info out of him. This might have nothing to do with our plan."

"Until we find out differently, let's just assume it does. When are you getting home?"

"As soon as I recover from the heart attack I'm about to have. Why?"

"I'll get some tacos from the place across the street you like."

"Call them and order it. On the food delivery burner phone. And make sure you check who's outside before you open the door."

"I'm not an amateur, Richard." JoJo hung up the phone and finished her smoke.

She sat at the table and eyed the envelope again.

JoJo had done countless cons on rich men, but they were always ones that ended when she got the money. The men were usually too embarrassed or too married to go to the police and make a complaint, so she was always in the clear.

This time it was different. She hadn't targeted Ernie Patek for his money, but for a piece of paper that may lead to more money than all her targets combined had.

The price for it? Ernie was not one to let something like this go. He was not going to go to the police, for sure, but he had other ways of trying to track her down. And now the cartel and DEA?

JoJo missed the days of fleecing a man and spending the next month or so binge watching television and eating junk food.

She stared at the envelope again. The tiny piece of paper that has brought all this weight down on her and Rick. In that moment she hated it. She hated that she went through with the plan. She didn't need the stress and she definitely didn't need a ton of people coming after her.

They were going to open it together, kind of a celebratory present for the first part of the job well done, but JoJo wasn't in the mood to celebrate.

She reached over and picked up the envelope, running her nail under the flap.

There it was inside. A folded piece of paper with the secret to untold riches.

JoJo pulled out the paper and began to unfold it. She frowned, but continued.

The paper hit the table as if it were a rock.

Blank.

The paper was blank.

No notes. No coordinates. Nothing but a sheet as white as her face probably was at the moment.

But she knew it had something on it. Ernie had flashed it at her a number of times, thinking he was funny and teasing her.

Rick was going to shit himself. He's out playing with that street rat while she was sitting here all the time with nothing but–

A memory flashed through JoJo's head.

The alley. The kids running by her. Nacho taking the opportunity to grab her ass.

A distraction. She was fooled by a little kid pulling a simple pickpocket misdirection.

Nacho must have switched envelopes.

"That little motherfucker."

TWENTY

Raul picked up his phone but dropped it back onto the table, wanting to scream. He'd returned to the villa to find Maria and Ernie had left, but no one could tell him where or why.

Was she coming back? Did she decide to move Ernie and do this on her own? It was her right, surely, but Raul knew she'd know how upset he'd be. The power struggle within the cartel was real enough, and this might tip the scales. Right now Raul and Maria were working together... but all it would take was a slight, and he'd have justification to take her out.

If I can find her, Raul thought. He was sure he could spend the next few hours wasting time talking to everyone in the house, but even if they finally told him where Maria and Ernie were, it would be too late.

It was better to sit and wait. Gather more intelligence in the meantime. Make sure his men were watching Alberto and any of the other boats on the docks that might play into this in the future. He'd need more men to throw a wider net, but knew Maria was the only one who could grant them.

If she was playing this out without Raul, there was no way she'd want even more men loyal to Raul in town.

He decided to gather everyone loyal to him here and start to make subtle plans so he wasn't caught unprepared. Best case was Maria and Ernie went for a ride, maybe a picnic, so she could coerce the man into telling her information. Worst case? There might be a sniper waiting for Raul to cross past an open window and take him out.

Raul decided to stay clear of the windows. He went into the kitchen, making sure two of his men were with him at all times, and had one of the women make him some tacos. He opened a couple of beers and sat in the formal living room, away from the window, while his food was prepared.

What do I know so far? Not much. The woman stole the map to a fabulous treasure. Ernie Patek likely has no clue where it is. Maria is trying to get the information from him and find the woman, same as me, Raul thought.

He smiled when his food was brought to him and asked for another beer since he'd already finished the two he'd brought with him. He worried he'd get so nervous he'd drink himself into a stupor. He decided one more drink wouldn't kill him before switching to something nonalcoholic.

Raul had left his phone in the other room and asked one of his men to bring it to him, a faint plan beginning to formulate while he ate.

He had no one loyal inside Maria's inner circle, which was bad. He should have been working on it for months. Instead, his arrogance of thinking he knew everything had come back to bite him on the ass. Now he was in the dark, until Maria decided to fill him in.

As soon as he got his phone back he checked but she hadn't called. No one had, in fact, which was upsetting. Raul had been all over town, spreading money or threats, looking for the mystery woman who'd stolen the map.

There should be some information headed his way, and it should have already arrived.

Unless this woman also had powerful friends and enough money and loyalty to keep everyone quiet.

Raul wondered if Maria knew this woman. It was entirely possible Maria was behind the theft of the map. It made sense. Why not? Raul knew his goal wasn't to hand it over to Maria when he got it from Ernie, it was to hold onto it, study and learn from it, before having a forgery made.

While Maria was off at a bogus location, Raul would quietly hire divers and a boat to dive on the real location. His goal was to get the treasure and stash it for a few months.

In the meantime, Maria would end up killing Ernie, thinking his map was a lie.

Maybe even think Ernie had lied about everything, Raul thought. *There was no treasure, no shipwreck... nothing but a fake map*.

It was a risky plan, and Raul wasn't sure he had enough men on his side to pull it off.

But for all of that treasure I need to try, Raul thought, finishing his food. He pointed at one of the men in the room with him, someone he wasn't sure he could completely trust. There were only a few he could trust without a thought. "I need agua de jamaica, please and thank you. Get a cold glass for you and your partner, too."

The man was off, back to the kitchen, while Raul went to the window but decided not to present a target. He fell onto a sofa and kicked off his shoes.

Where was Maria and Ernie?

He decided to stop playing this subtle game and take the bull by the horns. He called Maria.

When she answered on the fifth ring, Raul tried to remain calm. Pleasant. "When can I expect you back? I wanted to have the cooks begin a fabulous meal for you, Miss Guerrero."

There was a pause on the line. Raul heard wind, which could mean she was driving with the windows down. Or on water in a boat.

Had Ernie already told her where the treasure was, and they were on their way to claim it?

"I'm not sure if I'll be heading back that way. Going to another villa for the night, at least. There are things happening and I need some space to think," Maria said. "I'll be having a conference call soon, and you will need to be on it."

"Of course." Raul wondered what that actually meant. They never did group calls, especially when they weren't in secure locations. Another villa? There were several possibilities. Maria not coming back here meant things were moving at a rapid pace, or something very wrong or very good had occurred.

"Should I come to you? It might be safer to talk in person," Raul said.

Maria chuckled on the line. "The call is for several important people. I'm not sure you being at my side will make much of a difference. There's nothing major to report, Raul. Just a quick catch up. I'll need to know anything and everything you've seen or done today. I'd hate to lose more time on this, especially with the American woman still loose... unless you managed to capture her?"

"Not yet," Raul said firmly. He knew it was a dig from Maria because she'd taken the map on his watch, while he was supposed to be acquiring it.

"Then I will text you an hour before the call. Feel free to have my cooks make whatever you and my soldiers want, too." Maria disconnected the call.

And my loyal workers.

Raul frowned. Maria had definitely stressed those four words, letting Raul know who was in charge. Still in charge.

The play back and forth between them was beginning to heat up. This was not going to end well for either Raul or Maria.

Raul needed to make plans so he'd eventually come out on top.

"Thank you," he said when the man returned and handed him a cold drink.

TWENTY-ONE

Baker sat on the low-slung chair, his ass almost touching the sand. He took a sip from the straw sticking out of the coconut he'd bought at a stand behind him. It was a mix of fresh fruit juices and rum, but by the way the ocean seemed to ripple and sway, the drink must be mostly rum.

He'd turned away the people walking around with Aloe leaves and the others offering foot and back massages. Despite the beauty of some of the women offering to rub him, Baker didn't want anyone but his wife's hands on him. Sure he'd look at other women–nothing wrong with that–but he never strayed or even thought about it.

Suzanne was his world, and he was down here risking his life to try to save hers.

Despite this trip not being a vacation, this was the first time he felt like he could relax. At least for the afternoon.

Tailing the cartel was not only dangerous work, but extremely boring. Boredom led to mistakes, and mistakes down in this area usually meant death.

But now he had Alberto. Well, not quite yet, but Baker was pretty sure the boat captain would come around to his side.

Especially since Baker made it seem like he had the backing of the DEA behind him.

It was difficult enough being solo in this area, but if anyone found that out Baker would be screwed. He'd be one of those people you read about in the news who went down to Mexico on vacation and disappeared. The Mexicans had a word for it, but he couldn't remember what it was. Partly because of the rum pumping through his system, and partly because his Spanish was limited to greetings and asking where the bathroom was.

While Raul and his men had talked with Alberto, Baker sat in his car, far enough away to hopefully not be noticed, but close enough that his parabolic receiver could pick up most of what was said. The crashing of the waves overrode some of the conversation, but he got the gist of it.

He'd head back to the docks later in the day and put a little more pressure on Alberto. Nobody wanted to cross the cartel in this country, but the offer of protection from a U.S. agency was usually enough to persuade most people to gather and spill information.

Baker watched the Pacific waters break onto the beach and roll back into infinity. Did he feel bad lying to Alberto about being about to protect him? That his agency had his back?

Baker took a long sip from his coconut drink and felt a wave of relief wash through his body.

No. He didn't feel bad.

Alberto, whether one wanted to believe he'd gone straight or not, was a known drug runner. Who knows how much of that shit had gotten across the border into America? Drugs tainted with enough fentanyl to kill an elephant.

Alberto, a simple middleman, was just as guilty as the dealers on the streets who sold the drugs to the addicts. American addicts.

Baker could give less than a shit if the Mexicans wanted to kill themselves with pills and powder. But they should keep it in their own house and not bring it into his.

Baker sucked the rest of his drink out of the coconut, disappointed when he heard the gurgling of the last bit of liquid flowing up the straw. He tossed the empty coconut onto the sand beside him and sighed.

The sun was like a prize fighter beating down on his face and the only protection he had was the cool booze. But getting more would mean attempting to get out of the ridiculously low beach chair he had sunk into.

Here he was, in a place most people would call a paradise destination, and he was debating between making an effort to get another drink while his wife was alone at home dealing with a disease Baker couldn't begin to understand. But seeing her dealing with pain that broke through the patches and medication she was prescribed, watching her push through and force herself to live while she still had embers of life inside her–that was what made him feel guilty.

Fuck screwing over Alberto.

Baker had waited all his life to meet someone like Suzanne, and he was willing to do anything to keep that part of him alive. Before her, he wasn't even sure he was living. He was just doing the things he had to do to make it through each day.

She's getting eaten from the inside out, and I'm sitting here bitching about having to get up from a chair, Baker thought.

"Uno mas, señor?"

Baker jumped, as much as he could since he was almost ass deep in sand. He looked over his shoulder and saw another coconut drink and a hell of a lot of cleavage.

Out of all the beautiful women he'd watched walk by, this one must be the queen of them all. She looked like that chick in the George Clooney movie about vampires. He shifted his legs in an attempt to hide the growing bulge in his pants.

"Oh, um, uh, yes. Thank you." Baker reached into his shorts and pulled out a twenty dollar bill. "Do you have change?"

"No. No change, but what would be better than having a wonderful drink while getting a wonderful foot massage?"

Baker stifled a groan. Was a massage by a beautiful woman really a slight against his wife? It's not like he was going to have sex with her. And if there ever was someone to say yes to, it was this one.

Baker handed her the twenty and nodded, taking the coconut as she came around to face him. He glanced at her butt before she turned around. Her thong was halfway up her perfect bubble butt and he had to quickly adjust himself again, hoping he was able to hide his excitement.

She knelt down in front of him and pumped some lotion from a bottle that was clipped to a leather belt around her waist.

Baker took a deep pull from his drink and moaned as she began working on his rough, calloused feet.

The woman didn't say much, just made eye contact whenever he did, and smiled. He drank some more and grimaced as she pressed on a sensitive area, seeming to know exactly where his aches and pains were.

Behind him, he heard a couple car doors close. It was a shame. He had been enjoying his time alone on this long stretch of beach, even before this woman had shown up.

"What's this flavor?" Baker asked as he gulped down more than he should in one sip.

"Very special mix. Only for very special people."

Baker smiled and felt the rum run through him something fierce. It was really getting to his head.

He tried to tell her that she was doing a great job, that she made a really strong drink, that–

Shadows fell over him, blocking the sun.

The woman stopped her massage and stood up, her smile still a smile, but in a different way.

Baker slurred out a sentence, but even he couldn't understand what he said.

Then, nothing.

TWENTY-TWO

Cuba kept staring at her, and she didn't like it. She did, however, like the bottle of tequila he'd handed her as soon as they got into his boat and the full bottle Cuba handed her to replace the one she'd finished on the ride to shore.

"Where are we going?" Grace asked, seated next to Cuba, who was driving. His two friends were sitting behind them.

"To a safe place. Then we'll call your father and make our demands," Cuba said and smiled. He gently tapped Grace's kneecap. "Are you having a good vacation yet?"

"Peachy. My boyfriend was just killed in front of me and my father's boat sunk. What could be better?" Grace stifled her tears. Thinking about Nathan made her sad. Did she love him? Probably not. He was just another boy in a long line of boys she'd deal with in her life until she was done using them.

"You didn't love Nathan and he was too stupid to love you. Not properly," Cuba said. "I know these things."

"There are a lot of things I apparently don't know about you," Grace said. "Like the fact I thought you were my father's closest friend."

Cuba chuckled. "Friendship and money don't often go hand in hand. I love your father like a brother. We've been through so much together, but Ernie makes too many mistakes. Too much of his life choices have to do with appearances, with his gut instead of gathered intelligence. Reality. The man has always lived in a fantasy world of his own making."

"That all seems like a lame excuse to screw over my father," Grace said.

Cuba chuckled again. "And you may be right. In the grand scheme of things, though, I can justify my actions because your father does things to leave that door open. He thinks he's much smarter than he is. The man is lucky in everything he does." Cuba glanced at her as he drove. "Take you, for example."

"What about me?"

"It almost seems unfair that Ernie Patek should have such a wonderful daughter. What did he do to deserve that? Huh?" Cuba chuckled again.

Grace looked away. She felt very uncomfortable right now. Cuba had been like a second dad to her all these years. He'd been around forever, always helping his parents with things. She couldn't remember a time in her life when he wasn't around. He'd watched her grow up. Taught her how to ride a bicycle when her father was away on business. Looked after her mother all that time, too.

Was he hitting on her now? Gross. While Cuba was a good-looking man, this all felt strange. Not in a good way, either, like when she'd drop acid at a rave in London or when she'd eaten those mushrooms in Venice.

"I asked you where we were going," Grace said, turning back to Cuba. If he tried to force himself on her she'd fight tooth and nail. She reminded herself she was a strong, independent woman. She could handle anything and take care of herself.

"To a secure area right outside of town," Cuba said. "I told you this."

"No, you keep being vague about it. Why?"

Cuba was glancing in his rearview mirror a lot the last couple of miles.

Grace turned back in her seat. "Are we being followed? Is it my father?"

"I think we were but they turned off at some point, which means there is either another vehicle ahead that will pick us up, or they have other means to find us. Definitely too sophisticated to be your father." Cuba was staring up at the sky as he drove now. "Watch for drones."

"My father has drones?"

Cuba frowned and glanced at Grace. "No, your father has nothing except the keys to vast riches, which he doesn't deserve. Got it? The cartel, on the other hand, has a vast reach and they might be chasing after us. If they know we have you and you can be used to manipulate your father into handing over whatever intelligence he's actually gleaned... you are a prized possession, my dear. I'm keeping you safe from the cartel."

Grace laughed. "So... kidnapping me, killing Nathan and sinking the yacht is all to protect me? I don't believe this."

Cuba slapped the steering wheel, which frightened Grace. She'd never seen him lose his temper, even when she knew her father was annoying him with one bad idea after another.

"Nathan was working for the DEA. Do you get it? He was using you to get to your father. Nothing more. How convenient how you two met," Cuba said.

"Wait... what? No. Nathan and I..." Grace looked away again. They'd met because he had run into her a couple of times while she was on vacation in Toronto. First at that swanky bar, where he'd bought her a drink but acted mysterious and didn't talk to her. Then the next morning at the cafe, where he'd been seated at the next table. They'd ended up spending the next few days together, but he'd always been vague about when he was returning to the United States.

"Your father didn't know. He never liked Nathan but couldn't figure out why," Cuba said. "I figured out why. He'd meet with his handler every week. They were using you to get to your father, who they knew had a treasure map. Don't you see? No one is trustworthy, because whoever has the sunken treasure has so much wealth it will blow your damn mind."

"And you know where it is?" Grace asked.

"I certainly do, but I don't have the means or the team in place to retrieve it, which means someone else will have to do the dirty work and then I can swoop in and take it from them," Cuba said.

"What about my father?"

"What about him?"

Grace sighed. "He's putting a team together, right? He'll find this treasure and then... you'll kill my father?"

"No. Your father stupidly went to the cartel, thinking he could work with them and they'd be happy with a percentage," Cuba said, shaking his head. "They were going to kill him and take the map, but an unknown woman stole it first. Ernie had a side thing going while we were here. Have you ever seen her?"

"No. Maybe." Grace thought back to the days and nights they were here, but she'd barely seen her father. If he was staying with a certain woman she never cared or noticed. She knew her father paid professionals quite often, and Grace was always disgusted when she saw one of them. Her father tried to keep them away from her, which was at least something.

"Whoever she is… she has the map and knows the location, too." Cuba was still glancing at the sky for drones. "If your father had actually looked and memorized the map, he'd know, too. That makes at least three teams who know where the shipwreck is located. Not good, unless we can figure out how to get our hands on it, either because we find a suitable dive crew or we take it after their dive crew finds it."

"You know where it is?" Grace asked again.

Cuba nodded. "Yes, and so do you because you used my coordinates in the yacht. The yacht which we sunk on top of the shipwreck to slow everyone down while I figure this out."

TWENTY-THREE

Ignacio Morales – Nacho to the gringo he'd begrudgingly started to think of as a friend – never took the same path home. It was a habit he learned not from a father he never knew, or an older boy who taught him, but from the boxes of English spy novels he'd accumulated over time.

Most of what he learned and passed on to his gang came from books or lessons learned on the streets. But mostly from books.

He'd taught himself to read English and was more proficient at reading than speaking it. His crew thought he had some kind of sixth-sense for running the streets and dodging trouble, and that may be partially true. But the fact behind his seemingly uncanny ability to keep everyone flush and avoid the law was a simple rule of thumb: if it works for James Bond, it works for Ignacio.

He took an alley, barely wide enough to walk through, jumped a short wall halfway down, and crossed two backyards, dodging laundry on clotheslines and flipping off the people who yelled at him for invading their space.

Ignacio turned down another alley and took the fire escape to the roof. The buildings were so close together that it only took a minimum amount of effort to leap from one roof to another.

Ignacio made it through the maze and into his house.

"Mama," he called out.

"Hijo!"

Ignacio walked into the kitchen where his mother was cooking her usual pot of pozole. It was a smell he grew up with and made his mouth water no matter how many times he smelled it.

Ignacio took some money and put it in the jar where the rest of it went. Despite what they split between themselves, he always kept a little extra to bring home.

He went straight to the shower and washed off the grime from the street, as well as his feeling of being slimy from dealing with people he shouldn't be around.

His mama thought he was out playing with his friends another day, perhaps kicking around a makeshift ball made of old socks and rubber bands.

If she really knew what I was doing she'd be upset, he knew.

The rest of his day's earnings went into the hole in his mattress. He was close to needing another mattress to fill, but didn't know how to tell his mother how he'd acquired the money. He'd need to figure it out sooner than later, because he knew all of the new people in town were heading toward disaster.

The gringos paid well but the work was getting harder, especially when he was also dealing with the locals and the cartel and the occasional DEA agent who came through town.

He knew there was a new DEA agent lurking but so far he hadn't approached Ignacio or any of his gang.

If there was anyone close to a real-life James Bond in Mexico, it was a DEA agent, he supposed. He'd seen them in action, working with the local police – the few who weren't corrupt and in the cartel's pocket – and they didn't play around. They were nearly as ruthless as the cartel, which you probably had to be if you wanted to win this war.

Not that Ignacio really cared who won and who lost, as long as he could stay safe and keep collecting his fees.

He knew a couple of his crew were going to be dealt with soon, too. They'd been flouting the money lately, buying expensive clothing and acting like wannabe gangsters like they'd seen on the television, or dressing like they were junior cartel members.

Ignacio would need to get them together, tonight after dinner, in the abandoned church.

"I'll be right back, mama," he said after he washed his hands and face. The smell of food was making his mouth water and he looked forward to eating. Not lying to his mother about what he'd done today, though.

Ignacio stepped outside and caught the eye of one of his spotters on a roof on the next block. He gave a few simple hand signals, and the other boy nodded.

A meeting was set for tonight, just after dark.

Like a good, organized leader, Ignacio would need to see what they'd learned in the last couple of days. What angle they could use and who they could use it on. He never let his crew know everything he knew, but every bit of information from them needed to be told to the group.

Then plans could be made, and certain individuals could watch the many moving parts of this intricate dance.

Ignacio felt like a spy and smiled. He was the leader of a group of lowly street urchins, kids who were ignored. They could sidle up to anyone and no one would even notice, which definitely worked in their favor.

It meant any and all information was handed to them, and no one was any wiser.

Dinner was delicious, and his mother didn't ask too many questions. She'd smile as he talked and he got the feeling she knew part of what he was really doing but would never ask.

I'm doing it for you, Mama. I'm saving enough money we could move, maybe head into the United States and live like kings, Ignacio thought. He'd read many books with the setting of San Francisco or Los Angeles or New York. He wasn't a hundred percent sure where these cities were or how far they were from the dinner table, but they couldn't be too far away.

With enough money he figured they were all in reach.

He met up with his crew in the old church just after dark. He'd told his mother he was going to lie down and read for a bit, then slipped out the window and climbed the roofs a few blocks.

No one was dressed nicely, which was a good thing. He'd told them time after time they were street kids and needed to act like it. Dress like it. Be the dirty faces everyone ignored.

He knew which boys and girls had spent too much money on material items instead of on food for their families, and he was angry. Ignacio also knew better than to directly confront anyone, especially when they were in a group like this.

"We're getting sloppy," Ignacio finally said, making sure not to lock eyes with anyone he was indirectly addressing. "Too much bling, as the Americans say." He was distraught to see more than a few gold chains and silver crosses, rings and earrings that a typical street kid couldn't afford.

"If one of us is figured out, this entire operation goes down the drain," Ignacio said. "Starting tomorrow, anything of value gets left at home. We don't openly buy things, either. Most of us have friends and family not involved, who can buy fresh fruits and vegetables for our dinners. We use this money to help your mother and your father, not to show off. That will eventually get you and the rest of us... killed."

Ignacio gave a hard look to each and every member in the room. He received a few nods back but mostly blank stares.

They're getting soft. There's too much money coming in now, and hunger has been replaced with greed, he thought.

Ignacio knew something very big was about to happen.

He'd kept his ear to the ground and knew Rick and JoJo were after a sunken treasure, the same as the cartel. Likely the same as some of the boat captains. There was a definite buzz in town about it, and everyone was trying to get involved. Get their piece of the action.

Ignacio wanted his own fair share of it, too, and he was willing to sell this entire crew down the river if need be.

The treasure, whatever it actually was, could be his family's ticket out of Mexico.

TWENTY-FOUR

Grace stood in front of the picture window she had been told to avoid. She sipped on her third Tequila Sunrise of the day. Really, it was just a continuation from when she passed out to when she'd awoke this morning. Since Cuba had taken her and put a bullet in Nathan's head, Grace made the decision that the best course of action was to remain drunk during her kidnapping.

At least that way, she wouldn't care as much.

Grace had no idea where Cuba was. He'd taken off shortly after leaving her at this supposedly safe place with most of his men wandering around, making sure she couldn't escape. Mostly, they were staring at her body and thinking thoughts she didn't want to know about.

Grace snickered and shook her head.

This wasn't a safe spot. Every side of the house was open, no form of defense, easily accessible with the kind of men and firepower her father would bring down on this place once he found out where she was.

And Ernie Patek, as dumb as he could be, always found out what he needed.

Grace paced around the house, holding onto furniture and curtains when she needed to steady herself. There was a point where she wouldn't have minded Cuba taking her away from her father. But it was different this time. He was acting like an asshole. Also, even though she found him attractive, something about that felt off.

She walked up and down the carpeted steps, around the island in the kitchen, and weaved through the dozen pieces of equipment in the exercise room.

Could she wait for her father to find her, or would Cuba have the upper hand in this situation? Grace had a feeling Cuba would have no problem killing her and dumping her body far off into the Pacific for the sharks to tear apart.

Her father would find her, but he would probably need a little help, and Grace, as she continued to pace, thought of what she could do from this joke of a prison to send out that help.

To most of her friends and family back in California, she was the usual airheaded, blonde bimbo with barely enough brain cells to be able to remember her name. Grace hated the assumptions until she realized that being seen as stupid could come in handy in certain situations.

Nobody expected much out of her, for one. Her father gave her money every month and let her do pretty much whatever she wanted because he didn't think there was anything else she was capable of besides partying, tanning, and seemingly helpless when it came to anything besides enjoying herself.

But Grace always had an aptitude for picking things up very quickly and remembering events almost exactly as they happened, no matter how long ago.

Now, though with a good buzz on, Grace wandered the house not out of boredom, but to look to see what she could use to help get word out to her father. Some items were easier to find and grab than others. Some she needed to work at taking apart in between rounds around the house, or risk getting caught by one of the guards.

It was times like these where Grace was grateful that Ernie was her father and not some bigger asshole like Cuba.

Grace eventually made it back to her room, the booze starting to wear off a bit, which was partially why she took her time during her walk.

She pulled out all of the items she'd gathered and dropped them on her desk.

Using the side of her nail file, she cut down the length of PVC pipe to about six inches. Next, using the slippers in her vanity bag to cut and peel off the outer layer of the high-voltage inverter–the item that took her the longest to get.

She created a circuit with the three AAA batteries and battery housing, a switch, and the inverter. Grace wished she'd been able to also include a safety switch in case she accidentally triggered the homemade taser, but there wasn't anything she could do about that now.

After she finished the rest of the housing and everything was connected, she pressed the switch and held it against one of the metal legs of the desk. A strong blue light arced between the two small brass nails at the end of the pipe.

"Take that, MacGuyver."

By the time Grace had put everything together, gotten what she needed, and headed toward the back door, all she was wearing was a string bikini and a see-through shawl which did nothing but enhance the fact that she was nearly nude.

The taser was taped to the back of the shawl.

Grace dropped a small bag just out of sight of the sliding glass doors. Outside was a large expanse of lawn, decorated with exotic looking bushes and flowers, along with one very large, heavily armed man standing in front of her.

As far as Grace was able to tell from her laps around the house, there were five men on the property: one at the front door; two by the driveway; this dimwit out back; and someone on the roof. The last she knew because she could hear his pacing above her when she was in her room.

The roof guy was the only one she had to worry about besides this one who hadn't noticed her yet. But Grace was fairly sure that the guy would be concentrating more on the front than the back of the property. A mistake most dumb men with guns make: never covering their rear.

Grace slid open the door. Another mistake meatheads make is thinking that just because they have a gun, they shouldn't add an extra layer of security.

The guard heard the door slide and turned around. His face wasn't particularly mean looking, just temporarily pissed at having to stand in one spot in the Mexican sun.

The big guy held out his hand.

"Back inside." His voice sounded like he ate gravel and smoked road flares.

"Come on, I just need a little fresh air," Grace said, pushing her breasts toward him and loosening her shawl.

She smiled as his eyes darted down and quickly recovered. She assumed Cuba's punishment for letting her get away was worse than staring at her body.

"Can't do it. Back in."

Grace stood just outside the sliding glass doors and waited for what she knew was coming. When she didn't move, he took a step toward her, lowering his weapon and grabbing her arm.

She reached behind her and pulled out the homemade taser, jamming it into his crotch and pressing the switch.

Grace giggled as he went down, his face oddly the same as faces guys made when they orgasmed, except with a lot more pain in it.

She leaned over and tased him in his temple until he blacked out.

She grabbed her clothes out of the bag she had set aside and got dressed so she wouldn't have to run around in basically nothing.

Then, after grabbing his handgun, she began running across the backyard toward the tree line and hopefully to a town she was pretty sure was only a mile or so in that direction.

The easiest way to help her father out? Escape herself and then call him from a payphone – of which Mexico still had plenty.

Hopefully he wasn't too busy with that tramp to not answer the phone. Though knowing him since birth, Ernie Patek tended to always find a way to screw things up.

TWENTY-FIVE

Rick didn't want JoJo to leave the house, but she was never one to take orders from anyone. Especially not a man.

She was on a mission to find Nacho and the map. JoJo was pretty sure she told Rick something like, "I'm gonna find that asshole child and beat his ass across the country."

There had been very few people in her life who had screwed her over, and the ones who did paid for it at the end. She'd never really liked kids, and this was the perfect excuse to beat the crap out of one.

"You don't even know where he lives," Rick had said before she left. "And the fucking cartel is after you. Let me go."

"No way. You give that little shit too much leeway, and he'll probably wind up getting more money out of you and you'll get jack-shit, let alone the map that I worked so hard to get."

Now, as JoJo walked the streets, the brim of her cap pulled low, she wondered if Rick was right. Sure, they'd been expats, in this country and in this town for a long time, but finding a local who didn't want to be found would be close to impossible.

JoJo strolled around town, stopping at the usual spots she remembered Nacho hanging out at. The probably was, even though he ran a crew, Nacho had a unique ability to make you focus on him. She couldn't, for the life of her, remember the faces of the other kids who hung around him. They were like blurred heads in a nightmare.

Her plan, initially, was to find one of his other little shits and beat the crap out of him until he gave up where Nacho was. Now she realized, she might accidentally start wailing on some innocent child and not only have to worry about the cartel seeing her, but an angry parent tackling her like some Lucha Libre fight.

JoJo went down the usual paths she would bump into Nacho during the day. She didn't see any kids, let alone the king dickhead of kids. She guessed there was a possibility that, since he had stolen the map from her and they tended to see each other most times when they were out, he was either in hiding or already trying to get at the treasure.

If it was any other kid, JoJo wouldn't be worried about having the treasure taken out from under her, but Nacho was smart and could get things done better than most adults.

After too much time under the sun, JoJo gave up. Maybe she should have had Rick look for him. The kid always seemed to pop up when he was around. And she had to admit that she was a little antsy, looking around to make sure nobody from the cartel was following her.

JoJo took a seat under the awning of a cafe and ordered an iced coffee and a churro. She sat back and wiped her brow, happy to be out of the sun.

Maybe if I sit here the little shit will just walk right by, JoJo thought.

"Telephono? Pay ... phono. Phono dinero? Jesus fucking Christ does anybody speak American in this country?"

The voice reached JoJo halfway through her second churro. Some tourist being an asshole like usual.

The girl came into view. She was young and beautiful, even though her hair was a frizzy mess and she had sweat stains under her pits.

JoJo didn't want to admit it, but back in the day this girl would have given her a run for her money when it came to looks. JoJo would have won, of course. At least, that's what she told herself as she watched the girl walk under the awning and stop ten feet from her.

JoJo took a closer look at her. Everything she had on was designer. Even her hair, the mess that it currently was, had the look of a very expensive dye and cut job. She obviously came from money.

So what the hell is she doing walking around like a lunatic? JoJo thought.

"Do you have a phone in here?" the girl asked. The guy behind the counter shook his head and walked away. "Oh come on. This is a business. You have to have a fucking phone. Can I at least get some ice water? This weather is a son of a bitch."

The girl threw her arms up in disgust and turned toward JoJo. She glanced at her briefly, then looked again.

"Holy shit, are you American?"

"At one point, yes."

"Oh my god." The girl let out a sigh and slumped next to JoJo like a dog that's been walked too long. "You'd think there would be payphones all over the place here. Third World country, and all that."

"I'm pretty sure this isn't a third–"

"I mean, not a single one. And nobody seems to have a cell phone. Or they're just being assholes. Can I use your phone? Just for a minute. I need to call my dad."

"Are you in some sort of trouble? Lost?"

"I'm perfectly fine. What would make you say that?"

JoJo looked at the girl's sweaty face and general disheveled mess.

"No reason."

The girl stared at JoJo. JoJo stared back.

"So can I, or not?"

"Can you what?"

"Use your cell. You're American. Even the homeless have cell phones there."

JoJo was about to pull out her cell but thought twice. She didn't need her burner number showing up on some random guy's phone. Even though it would probably lead to nothing, it was better to be extra cautious than to be in jail or worse.

"I'm sorry, I don't have it on me. I live right down the road, so I didn't think to bring it. Why don't you let me talk to this guy here. I come here a lot. I can probably talk him into letting you use the phone."

"I'd appreciate it. Thank you. I'm Grace, by the way." The girl held out her hand.

"JoJo." They shook hands, as if they were going to know each other any longer than it took for the girl to make a call.

"JoJo Dancer, your life is calling," Grace said.

JoJo smirked. "Aren't you a little too young to know that movie?"

"Nobody is too young to not know Richard Pryor." Grace pointed to the melting ice and left over coffee. "Can I have that? I'm dying of thirst."

"Sure." JoJo began to turn to the counter.

"So that's not actually your last name, right?" Grace asked.

"What?"

"Dancer. I'm assuming you're not named after the movie."

"No. Definitely not."

"That's a shame. It's a cool last name to have. Better than fucking Patek. Dumbass name I had to get saddled with." The girl chugged the iced coffee dregs and chewed the ice.

JoJo paused as she was turning to the counter again.

There's no way. This girl couldn't possibly be Ernie Patek's daughter. Her mother must have the looks in the family.

Then JoJo thought of the map. The asshole kid. How she may never see the map again, but now she had something she might be able to use as leverage: Patek's kid. And who knows, maybe Daddy liked to tell her stories about sunken treasure.

"You know what? I mentioned I live right down the road. Why don't you come with me? I have a house phone and plenty of ice to chew on. You can call your father from there. In air conditioning."

"Oh my god, yes. Thank you. I need to get out of this awful heat."

JoJo helped Grace out of the seat and led her to her house. She'd have to figure out how to tell Rick why she brought the girl home without Grace hearing.

And JoJo would have to make sure Grace didn't get the chance to call Ernie Patek. At least, not right away.

TWENTY-SIX

Ernie knew that they knew. He didn't know where the treasure was, only a vague idea.

In the water is not a vague idea, he thought.

Maria kept looking at him and for once Ernie wasn't trying to flirt with a woman, which told him how much trouble he was really in. Sure, he'd been with women who were gold-diggers and only after his wealth, but he figured that was the price to pay for a pretty woman on your arm and in your bed.

This was another level, where he could lose his life. Not a good thing by any stretch.

"How many people work for you?" Maria asked, breaking the silence and taking Ernie mercifully away from his morbid thoughts of dying.

Ernie smiled at her and shrugged. "Hundreds. I run a lot of different businesses, both in America and overseas and–"

"No, idiot. How many people are with you in Mexico right now? Who will be looking for you?" Maria asked and frowned. "And don't even attempt to lie."

Ernie decided to tell the truth because he had nothing to gain. It wasn't like anyone knew about the map and the treasure but him, anyway. He hadn't even told his most loyal friend about it.

"My daughter and her boyfriend are here, enjoying the yacht, obviously."

"The boat wasn't where it was supposed to be and neither were they," Maria said.

Ernie shook his head. "It's a yacht, not a boat. Much bigger and more luxurious. Someday you and I can enjoy it together."

"I own six yachts, all likely bigger than the dinghy you own. Who else?"

Ernie frowned. "Cuba Zayas. My right-hand man. He doesn't know about the treasure, though."

"I told you not to lie."

"No, no, seriously... I didn't tell him. I told no one. I wanted to do this on my own, which is why I contacted the cartel and Raul to begin with. According to my daughter and Cuba, I'm here on vacation. Cuba wanted to come because he said he might have family in the area or something. I dunno. I haven't seen him in a few days. He comes and goes, you know? His own man and all that." Ernie lifted the sweating glass of beer and downed half of it.

"Only those three?"

Ernie shrugged again. "Cuba might have picked up a couple of men to work with us. Protection detail. I told him I didn't need it, I was trying to keep a low profile. I know he had at least two others with him the last we talked, but he said he was heading for Mexico City to relax."

"Call him. See what he's currently doing," Maria said. "We'll eventually find your daughter and her boyfriend. Those two I am not worried about."

"Yeah, sure. I just need my phone, which you took from me," Ernie said.

"If you tip him off to your location or that you're in trouble, I will personally shoot you in the face. You do not want to know what my men will do to your daughter, either." Maria handed Ernie his phone and drew a small pistol from the cushions on the couch she was seated at.

Ernie smiled, trying to make a joke and not get too flustered. "Does all of your furniture come pre-assembled with weapons inside? Or is that a cartel-only purchase?"

"Call this Cuba person. Now."

Ernie called Cuba.

"Speakerphone," Maria said.

Ernie did as he was told, listening as the phone rang over and over.

"Maybe he's taking a nap," Ernie said.

Maria leaned forward. "Maybe you're wasting my time."

"Hello?" It was Cuba and he sounded annoyed.

"Hey, it's me, Ernie. How's it going?"

"I'm a little busy right now. Can I call you back?"

Maria shook her head.

"I was wondering what you were doing, where you were. I'd like to meet up and get some dinner tonight," Ernie said and smiled at Maria, improvising.

Maria nodded her head.

"Sure. I can be back in town in a few hours. You tell me when and where we can meet. I'd love to know how your trip is going so far, my friend," Cuba said. "We have a lot to catch up on, I think."

"Yes, we definitely do." Ernie covered the phone and stared at Maria. He didn't know what to say next.

"Tell him you'll text an address to a restaurant soon and a time."

Ernie nodded and relayed the message to Cuba.

"Then I will see you then," Cuba said but didn't hang up the phone. "Uh, have you talked to Grace lately?"

"Grace? No. The weirdest thing happened, though–"

Maria placed the weapon on Ernie's nose and shook her head.

"What happened?" Cuba asked.

"Oh, she took the yacht out on her own, I guess. I haven't heard from her in hours, though," Ernie said and smiled at Maria, hoping he wasn't going to get his nose blown off. "Have you heard from her and Nathan?"

"No, can't say I have. I'm sure they're fine. You know your daughter. Always involved in some grand scheme or another. They likely fell asleep sunbathing and will be home late tonight looking like lobsters. Am I right? Grace does her own thing," Cuba said.

"Yes, she does. Okay, I will see you tonight," Ernie said.

Maria took the phone and disconnected.

"Now what?" Ernie asked.

"Now we wait. You need to shower because you stink of sweat and fear. New clothes for you, too. The garish outfits you wear for a man your size are ridiculous. You need more muted colors and less dumb Hawaiian shirts. And a man wearing open-toes sandals is not a real man," Maria said.

Ernie nodded and smiled. "I need a good woman in my life to show me the proper fashion."

Maria had the gun to his nose again as she stood. "You'll be really lucky to survive the next couple of days, never mind worrying about fashion and women. Understand me, gringo? If I were you I'd keep my mouth shut unless asked a direct question, and do everything I say to do tonight when you meet your friend Cuba."

"Fine," was all Ernie could manage. He was fearful of the anger in Maria's beautiful eyes and knew she was not bluffing. She'd killed before and she'd kill him without another thought.

"I'll have someone bring you clothes and another beer or two so you can relax. Now go shower," Maria said, turning and walking out the door.

Ernie watched her gorgeous ass shake as she moved, knowing he'd never get anywhere near it.

Knowing he was in trouble, but maybe his good friend Cuba would be able to save him.

TWENTY-SEVEN

Cuba hated cell phones for two reasons. If someone knew your number, they could get a hold of you no matter where you were or what you were doing. The second reason was because he couldn't slam a cellphone down, like a good old-fashioned phone handle into the receiver. The most he could do is throw it across the room. Then, he'd need a new phone.

Fucking technology.

Instead of reacting without thinking – something he'd been working on changing in his life – he took a deep breath, pretended to be calm, and put the cell in his pocket.

Then he slammed the stock of the AR-15 he held into the wall, demolishing the sheetrock and almost punching through to the outside.

When he had gotten back to the safe house, he knew something was wrong. The men guarding the entrance stepped aside as he drove through, but seemed like they wanted to look anywhere but in his direction.

And there was no guard on the roof.

His men knew better than to leave their posts. They'd seen what happened to others who did, so the only explanation for the unguarded roof was that something so big had happened that it overrode the fear of disobedience.

Cuba knew it had to do with Grace. Who else could it be? But he didn't know what exactly happened until he walked in and saw one of his men sitting on the couch with an ice pack on his nuts, looking like he'd gotten clocked in the head by Mike Tyson.

"Bitch caught me off guard. Tased my fucking balls. My head. There was nothing I could do. How was I supposed to know she was some sort of Mr. Wizard with technology? Fucking bitch."

Cuba nodded and grabbed the ice pack of the man's crotch. It was still mostly hard, only slightly melted.

He took it in his fist and slammed it against the man's nose. He heard a loud crack and blood poured out of the guard's nose like someone had turned on a faucet.

The guard cursed and held his nose, as if that would stop the torrent of blood.

"Where is this taser? Did she take it or drop it?" Cuba asked.

The guard who had been assigned roof duty pulled it out of the back of his pocket and handed it to Cuba.

Cuba smirked as he looked at the hastily put together device. No daughter of Ernie Patek could come up with something like this. That entire family were idiots. Only Cuba's daughter would be smart enough to figure a way out of her situation.

Even though Cuba was angry at the situation he found himself in, he was still able to let a little pride come through.

Maybe one day, when Grace learned the truth, they could work together. Cuba knew, as long as his plans went without another hitch and as long as Grace didn't try to contact Ernie before they found her, that time would come soon. And Ernie would no longer be around to act as a pretend leader.

But one thing at a time.

Initially, Cuba was going to use Grace as leverage against Ernie. The pathetic asshole knew she wasn't his daughter, but he also knew that Cuba had no problems following through on his threats – even if it meant killing Grace.

Now, with Grace gone, plans needed to shift. One of many things Cuba learned growing up in the environment he had lived in was that the ability to change paths without hesitation was just as important to survival as weapons, money, and intimidation.

Cuba looked at his man on the couch, still bleeding and dazed.

"Open your mouth," Cuba said.

The guard began begging immediately, something Cuba hated more than anything. If you came into this life as a man, have the decency to go out of it like one.

Cuba waited for the guard to say something that got his mouth open wide enough and shoved the homemade taser in it and pressed the button.

There was something amusing about how the guard danced around on the couch, eyes rolling around like a pair of those googly eye glasses.

Cuba pulled the taser out after getting a good chuckle in and shot the guard twice in the head.

"She's going to town. See if you can find her. Leave your weapons. The only people who carry weapons around town are the cartel. And Ernie was already stupid enough to get involved with them. I don't need that shit on me too."

The men left and Cuba sat, staring at the dead man ahead of him.

He would have gone after Grace as well, but there was no point. His three men would find her or they wouldn't. And if they didn't, his presence wouldn't help.

He thought back to growing up in The States, a tiny Puerto Rican boy in a big city that ate weakness and shat it out.

Most kids thought he was Cuban simply because of his name. Never mind how many times he tried to explain that his mother named him that because she loved the island. Once you were branded as not fitting in, there was no talking your way into the group. There was only fighting.

Cuba had taken his fair share of beatings growing up, until he learned how to fight dirty, how to use psychology to tear the other person down. How to use a curb as a head cracker.

Then he had his growth spurt, spent most hours at the boxing gym, lifting weights and tearing down opponents. Soon, he was running those streets he had once hid from.

Since then, he never looked back. He learned from those he deemed worthy of learning from, and ate the rest, just like the city.

Grace had grown up in the exact opposite manner Cuba had. She didn't want for anything. She was never afraid to step outside her giant house. She didn't have to fight to get what was hers.

But she had all of that in her, because she was his daughter. He saw it in her eyes when Ernie had held her up for him to look at after she was born.

Grace was a killer hiding in a spoiled rich girl's body. The best disguise a person could have who wanted to take over the world.

One day, Cuba thought. *One day soon she will know everything*.

Cuba stood up and looked at the guard with the fucked up face and swollen balls. He should have had his men take the body somewhere out of sight before they left.

But whatever. It didn't matter. Nobody was walking into this house anyway.

Cuba headed to the master bedroom to strip and take a shower. He wanted to look presentable, more suave and sophisticated than Ernie when they met up.

Cuba wasn't so stupid that he couldn't tell when he was on speaker phone. Obviously, Ernie was either in trouble and being told what to say, or he'd somehow charmed the cartel to his side and was legitimately trying to get Cuba in so they could discuss next steps.

Cuba was betting on this first option.

And he would be ready for whatever needed to be done tonight, in public or not.

TWENTY-EIGHT

He'd done another set of pushups and thought he was going to die, but Rick knew better than to stop. The Itch was so intense and he knew if he stopped trying to distract himself he'd need to Scratch.

As soon as JoJo returned with the cute twenty-something in tow, he knew things had changed. He was curious if it was for the better, though.

Rick grunted a hello and dropped down to do more pushups.

"What's wrong with the old guy? He some kinda fitness nut? He your boyfriend?" The new girl sat down at the table near the window and crossed her legs, but not before Rick had a good crotch shot.

JoJo kicked him lightly, letting her know she'd seen where his eyes had gone.

He rolled onto his back and smiled, lifting onto his elbows. "Hello, young lady. I am not a fitness nut, as my friend here will tell you. In fact, I'm mostly bored these days. Do what do I owe the pleasure of your appearance in my humble abode?"

The girl smiled. "Humble? This is actually pretty dirty. Falling apart."

Rick sat up and stared at JoJo. "Can you and I have a private conversation?"

"Eventually," JoJo said, pointing at the girl. "This is Grace. Say hi, Grace."

"Hi, Grace," the girl said and chuckled, as if that was funny.

"Grace, huh? And a fellow American." Rick got up off the floor and sat across from Grace. "I'm wondering what brings you to this armpit of the world."

Grace glanced at JoJo. "My father. I'm going to guess you know him, though... I don't really believe in coincidences. There's no reason so many Americans are in this tiny little shithole at once. I think you know my old man."

JoJo opened the small fridge and took out three bottles of water, passing them around. "Maybe this is all a coincidence, like you walking up to my table today."

"Ernie Patek," Grace said and smiled. She pointed at Rick. "You flinched. You know him. Of course you do."

"I've heard the name," Rick lied. "Do you need our help in reuniting you and daddy dearest. Is that what's going on?" He tried not to look directly at JoJo because he might lose it on her. This was completely unacceptable and could cost them their lives.

"Right now I need to find a friend or two, someone who can protect me," Grace said. She looked at Rick and then JoJo. "I can pay, of course."

"Cash? Right now?" Rick tapped the worn table top with a finger. "How much?"

Grace smiled. "Daddy is good for it."

Rick shook his head and stood. "Be right back. Don't go anywhere." He walked by JoJo, hooking her arm and leading her into the hallway.

JoJo was smiling. "I know, but what was I supposed to do? She walked right up to me like a stray dog."

"This is a setup," Rick said. "Her father is looking for us. An entire cartel, too. Nacho screwed us over as well. There's no way we can trust Alberto or any captain, either. We are screwed. How did this chick manage to locate you so easily?"

"This is fate. Don't you get it? We keep her under wraps and use her as a bargaining chip if need be," JoJo said.

"Playing with fire on this, my dear. We're not even sure who the players are at this point. I know we're not." Rick groaned. "My brain, the part that is usually quiet, the side that should talk sense all the time, is telling me to cut our losses and run. We've been defeated before this even began."

JoJo shook her head. "You're wrong. Completely talking out of the wrong side of your mouth. We got this. How many times have we been backed against the wall, huh? Many, many times. We made a promise we swore we'd always remember."

Rick laughed. "No retreat, baby, no surrender."

"Hey, if it works for Springsteen it's gotta work for us, right?" JoJo kissed Rick on the cheek and went back into the room.

Rick was expecting Grace to be halfway out the window, but she was drinking the bottled water.

He sat down across from Grace again and downed half his own water bottle. "Why are you here?"

"In Mexico?" Grace asked.

"No, in the universe. I'm asking a philosophical question." Rick felt his control slipping away.

Grace laughed. "A man and a woman had sex. I was conceived. Should I explain how procreation works, or think you have a basic idea about it, old man?"

JoJo wisely stepped between them, putting her hands on the table. "Stop with the sarcasm, Grace. We're wasting a lot of time."

"I'm here on vacation. Nathan and I came down with my father. While he was off with his whores we took the yacht out to get some sun, but then..." Grace looked down at her hands in her lap. "I don't want to talk about it."

"But you have to, see? Unless we know all about your reasons here, we can't help you," Rick said, wanting to grab her by the shoulders and shake her. He needed a fix or more exercise.

Grace looked at JoJo. "Cuba found us. The anchor was stuck on a shipwreck. He shot Nathan and sank the yacht. Kidnapped me."

"The country of Cuba did that?" Rick asked.

"No, you moron. Cuba Zayas. He's my father's right hand man, but he's really against my dad. I know it now. He was trying to use me to get to my father and get what my father really came down to Mexico for, which wasn't just about Mexican whores."

"Then what was it about?" JoJo asked.

"Money. Always about money." Grace sighed. "He killed Nathan, even though Nathan didn't do anything."

"Whos' Nathan?" Rick asked.

"He was my boyfriend. Not the love of my life or anything, but still a decent guy," Grace said.

Rick pointed a finger at Grace. "You said the anchor was caught on a shipwreck." He glanced at JoJo and smiled. That was also not a coincidence. What was the chance of that happening, and being the shipwreck they were looking for?

"Yeah. Cuba seemed to be pissed about it, too. He was mad we'd gone to the spot and that's why he sank the yacht, I guess." Grace shrugged. "I need to find my father and see if he'll get us out of Mexico. I just want to go home. Or maybe to Paris."

Rick stood again. He was going to grab JoJo by the arm and take her back into the hallway, but JoJo shook her head.

"You can stay with us and we'll help you find your father," JoJo said to Grace. "Cuba might be looking for you and he seems like he'd hurt you."

"No, I doubt he'd actually hurt me," Grace said and smiled. "He's my biological father. Only I'm not supposed to know that."

TWENTY-NINE

Alberto had no idea why he was sitting across from this kid. Granted, most people in town knew who Ignacio was. Probably another degenerate who would grow up to run shit around here.

But now, he was still a street rat. The only reason he was entertaining him was because of the map that was laid out on the table in front of him.

"You bring me there, you get a quarter of the money."

"Really? A whole quarter? For bringing you somewhere you can't get to on your own, with my ship and my fuel. Also, who's going to go down there? How much diving experience do you have? Do you know how to get the treasure up from the bottom, or were you just planning on stuffing it into your little swim trunks and drowning yourself?"

"I'm not stupid."

"I'm not saying you are. I'm saying you haven't thought anything through. You're money blind. So, let's say I do agree to do this. I'm doing it for less than half, plus the cost of running the boat, the Nitrox I'll probably have to use considering how long I'll need to be down there. You see where I'm going with this?"

Ignacio nodded. "Yes. Ripping me off."

Alberto tapped the map.

"Where'd you get this?"

"Found it."

"Found it?"

"Yes. Found it in the garbage."

Alberto picked up the map and folded it up along the crease lines. He handed it to Ignacio. The kid was smart, but the kind of child smartness that equaled adult stupidity. He was also an annoying little shit.

"I don't care what you do with that, but my advice would be to keep it out of sight and maybe drop it back off to who you stole it from. Slip it under their door. Whatever. Just get it out of your possession."

Ignacio gave Alberto a look that was probably meant to intimidate. But Alberto had been in the kid's same place when he was young and he wasn't easily rattled. He knew Ignacio wasn't going to get rid of the map, but he was trying to talk him into being safe, one street kid to another.

The only problem was that Alberto was no longer a street rat. And when he thought back to how he would have reacted to some adult telling him what to do, he knew what Ignacio would do.

"I know you're working with JoJo and Senor Rick. Rick is an idiot and shares too much with me. But how are you going to work with them when they don't even know where the treasure is? I have it right here." Ignacio waved the map. "I have a guarantee. What are they offering you except an idea with no directions?"

Alberto looked around, expecting Raul or one of his men to be off in the distance watching them. While he wasn't sure, Alberto had backed Raul off of him the last time they met. At least, temporarily.

They knew each other too well, and Raul would even circle around back to him. Most of the other local charter captains didn't have the experience, and more importantly didn't have the balls to do anything but throw fake smiles at the tourists and try to stay out of trouble with the cartel.

He also didn't need that DEA guy, Buster or Banker, or whatever the hell his name was spotting him sitting with Ignacio while he waved an actual treasure map in the air like a flag of war.

"I have it," Ignacio was saying as Alberto came out of his thoughts. " I have the solution. I have where it is. Those gringos have nothing and they were stupid enough to let me take it from them and then point me right to you."

Alberto grabbed Ignacio's arm and slammed it down on the table. The kid winced and then tried to throw a punch at him.

Alberto easily dodged it.

"Keep your voice and this fucking map down. You're a walking invitation to get both of us killed."

"Psst. I'd like to see them try. Me and my crew, we're going to run things one day. Not Raul, not anybody else."

"Sometimes things don't work out as you plan."

Alberto signaled for a beer and leaned back on the wobbly chair. He stared out at the ocean, a place where he was the most comfortable. The steady ground under his feet was what made him feel nauseous, not the rocking of a boat.

He was at an impasse. If he turned the kid down, he'd just run to someone else, flashing that map around like an idiot. Eventually, the cartel or someone else would catch up to him, probably kill him, and take the map.

If he agreed to take on the job, he'd be betraying JoJo and Rick, and would also need to do all the hard work himself. Did he really trust Ignacio and a bunch of his crew on his boat while he was down who knows how many feet underwater?

Alberto grabbed his beer and left some money on the counter.

"Come on. Let's go."

"Go where? We're not ready yet."

"Not to get the treasure. Just to the boat. I need to make sure I have a wetsuit that will fit you. Then I'm going to have to give you a crash course in diving. I don't need you all the way down with me, but I'll need you halfway, which means you're getting in the water. Got it?"

Ignacio looked like he didn't like that idea at all, but he nodded his head and followed Alberto out to the docks.

Alberto chugged the beer as they walked down the slip toward his boat.

"You nervous, old man?" Ignacio asked, smirking. "Need some liquid courage?"

"Too hot out here. By the time we got to the boat, this would be warm piss water."

They walked up alongside the boat and Ignacio put a foot on the side. Alberto pressed a hand against his chest and pushed him back on the dock.

"First, never get on anyone's boat without asking permission. That is rule number one."

"What's rule number two?"

"Whatever I tell you to do, you do. No questions. No smart remarks. The ocean is not like the street. The water will swallow you faster. Now get onboard."

Alberto waited for Ignacio to hop on before following him. He finished the rest of the beer just as Ignacio turned around, probably to ask another stupid question.

Alberto never got to hear what it was.

As Ignacio turned, he swung the empty bottle at the kid's temple.

Ignacio dropped like someone had flipped his off switch.

Alberto looked around, but nobody was close by. He grabbed the kid's arms and dragged him down the stairs to the cabin below.

He had no plan from here. He just knew he couldn't let the kid leave his sight and he definitely wasn't going to go treasure hunting for him.

As he tied Ignacio up, he saw the map sticking out of his pocket.

The real question now: take the map and go out himself, or make a call to JoJo and Rick?

Alberto didn't know the conditions he'd be under, or if he'd need a few extra hands.

"No harm checking, though," Alberto said. "Can't be any harm in that."

THIRTY

The light shining in Baker's eyes was unbearable. Even with his eyes closed, the heat and the force of it penetrated into his brain.

"Where am I? Who are you?" Baker had noticed there were shapes in the room with him.

"I could ask the same questions but I already know the answer. Take the light from his face so the gringo can properly see who he is dealing with."

When Baker felt the light move away from his face he opened his eyes and blinked a few times. He saw spots for nearly a minute.

His arms and legs were tied to a heavy chair in the middle of a room. A nice room, actually. He was expecting cement floors and walls, dripping brown water from the ceiling. Rats scurrying through the garbage and bones.

Instead, he was in a palatial great room. There was a piano in the far corner and a full liquor cabinet. Thick rugs on the floor. Paintings on the walls.

Six well-armed men, too.

"I'm Raul Santiago, but you must know that already, Mister DEA agent."

Baker knew he was in trouble.

"Why shouldn't we kill you now and dump your body outside of town? Huh?" Raul pulled up a chair and sat down across from Baker. He was smiling. "Did you think you'd get away with spying on us without repercussions?"

"I'm not spying on anyone. I'm on vacation," Baker said.

Raul laughed and so did his men a second later.

"I want to know where the rest of your team is," Raul said. "They are good at hiding. Like, uh... Bigfoot, no? They are somewhere nearby and we need to find them."

"I am alone. Check the flight records," Baker said. He knew they'd never believe him. He needed to change tactics. "Fine. I'm part of a team. If I don't call in soon they'll know I was captured. They'll use every means necessary to locate me. I'm an agent of the United States government."

Raul put up a finger. "Ahh, but this isn't the United States. This is Mexico, gringo. We have our own rules and our own government, which the cartel mostly controls. So... you have no authority here, and even if you thought you did, you were wrong. Dead wrong."

"I hope you can fight off an entire platoon of Navy SEALS, because that's what will be looking for me," Baker said.

Raul shrugged. "I guess we'll see, right? I've always wanted to kill your elite fighters. This will be good practice for us. We get to shoot real American heroes. Maybe it will show the people above me that the United States is nothing and we need to stop cowering and take the fight to the border and beyond." Raul stood. "Maybe once we conquer your country they'll let me have Texas. Or better yet, Las Vegas."

"Las Vegas is not a state, it's a city," Baker said. He knew he was pushing it but this cartel idiot was pissing him off. "I wonder how you're going to feel when the order is given to come in and rescue me."

"Maybe there won't be anyone to rescue," Raul said. He pulled the Glock from his waistband and put the muzzle against Baker's forehead. "They might come in, guns blazing, and find your corpse or pieces of you strewn about. Who can say?"

"If you kill a DEA agent there will be no rest until you're dead and gone," Baker said. "You know it and your bosses know it."

"Maybe." Raul started to pace around the room. "It could be worth the risk, though. It would definitely give street credibility to me and my men."

Baker chuckled. "It will definitely make you all heroes and martyrs when they parade your lifeless corpses through town, right? That's the only way this will end."

"Then I should let you go?" Raul was in Baker's face now. "Untie you and see you on your merry way? I think we are past that."

Baker knew he needed to play this cool. He certainly didn't want to die today. He was here for his wife and he needed to focus on that part of this. All of it was a risk. "We are after the same thing, you and I. Perhaps we can work together."

Raul shook his head. "I highly doubt that."

"Which part? Do we want the same thing or do we work together?" Baker asked.

Raul frowned. "Tell me what we both want."

"Treasure," Baker said.

Raul smiled. "What do you know about treasure, huh?"

"I know there is a shipwreck out there, nearby, and everyone seems to know about it but not the exact location." Baker took a deep breath. He knew this could go a number of ways, most of them bad for him. "With my reach I can find out where it is. Who knows and who can do the dive for us."

"I can do that myself," Raul said.

Baker shook his head. "Can you? If it were possible you would've done it already, I think. No. We need to work together."

"And what do you get out of this, gringo?"

"My fair share. That's all I want," Baker said. "I can keep the rest of the DEA team at bay, but I need some assurances from you."

Raul started pacing again, faster around the room. He finally stopped in front of Baker and sat back down. "We can work together but you will not be able to get away from me. You are my prisoner until the treasure is found and split. Then you go your own way. Deal?"

"Deal. I'd shake on it but my hands are tied," Baker said. He knew he was making a deal with the Devil but he had no choice. He knew Raul would put a bullet in his head as soon as Baker was no longer useful, but this gave him a few more days to live and figure out a plan.

There were others in town also looking for the treasure, and he'd need to align himself with any of them if possible. Strength in numbers.

Baker smiled when Raul had one of his men cut Baker loose.

"How will you get in touch with the DEA so they don't swarm us and lose their lives?" Raul asked.

"I need my phone. There are certain things I need to say," Baker said.

"I don't trust you."

Baker shrugged. "And I certainly don't trust you. But this is the world we currently live in." He put out his hand. "My phone?"

Raul handed over the phone. "If this is a trick–"

"Then you're all dead. But it is not." Baker dialed his wife's number and she answered on the first ring. "Hey, honey. Just checking in. Got busy at work and didn't have time to call. Yes, yes, meeting after meeting. I'll be home soon. No, nothing to worry about. Just another boring day doing paperwork as an agent. Oh, she did? I hope you told your sister I said hi. Yes, a cruise sounds wonderful once you're better."

When Baker disconnected he put the phone in his pocket, but Raul took it from him.

"I hope that wasn't letting them know where we were, as if you know," Raul said. He glanced at Baker's phone. "Just in case..." He popped open the phone and took out the battery and the SIM card. "I'll keep this with me at all times."

Baker had no idea what he was going to do next. It felt like he'd fallen out of the frying pan and into the fire.

THIRTY-ONE

Grace heard the couple whispering in the other room. There was no better way to let someone know you were talking about them than to whisper.

There were a few things Grace put together since the older woman had brought her here. They knew who she was, or at least who her father was. And they knew why her father was here. For a moment Grace thought about Nate. The look on his face as Cuba killed him.

Grace shrugged off the thought. While she wasn't super fond of Nate – just another boy toy for however long she deemed fit – Grace was not a cold-blooded killer. Seeing something like that happen right in front of her was traumatic.

But she was resilient. She could compartmentalize when needed, and now was the time to not think about the past.

The other thing Grace put together from watching how the two interacted, was that they'd had a lot of experience on the wrong side of the law and seemed afraid of something. What? Grace didn't know. If they were at all involved with her father, then that meant they may also have an issue with the cartel. And around here, when people looked afraid, it was usually because of the cartel.

Grace chuckled.

She'd escaped one prison only to find herself in this position. Sure, she could just stand up and walk out the door. They hadn't tied her to the chair or anything. But Grace was certain that the moment she stood, they'd come out from their secret meeting, all smiles, and try to coax her into staying.

When JoJo had brought her in, the old guy – who looked like he was jonesing for something – gave Grace a strange look and then JoJo a stranger one.

JoJo introduced the two, explaining Grace's situation. She made an emphasis on her last name, the first moment Grace realized something was off.

She'd looked around the small, but cozy apartment and didn't see a house phone anywhere. That was the second hint something wasn't right.

And of course now, being left alone for the last few minutes while they talked about her in the other room was strike three.

Grace sipped some water and focused on the grain of the table in front of her. This was something she did whenever she really needed to think about a situation. She'd find something to stare at that was static and uninteresting and zone out on it until her vision blurred and it felt like her brain was working overtime.

Grace didn't think they planned on letting her call her father. At least, not until they came up with some sort of plan to get whatever it was they wanted from him.

The treasure. Of course it's the treasure. Ernie Patek had a lot of money, but nothing close to what this treasure was supposed to be.

Grace had heard of it a few times when she was younger, thinking he was just making up a story for her to fall asleep to. But as the years went on, she overheard too many conversations between her father and people he knew, or Cuba and her father, for the treasure to be just a story.

Then he'd invited her and Nate down to come vacation. Why would he need her down here when he obviously wasn't going to bring her in on salvaging whatever was underwater?

A cover story? He was just down here with family on a simple vacation. No, that didn't make sense.

Distraction. He never liked Nate, and the feeling was mutual. He invited her and Nate down to be a distraction to whoever he was trying to partner up with. He knew they'd take the boat out, and the people watching would most likely have to split up, some following her and Nate.

That was what she was to him. A big fucking distraction so he could get what he wanted. Had she ever been anything different?

Somewhere in the background, breaking through the barrier she'd put up between the real world and her head, a phone rang.

Grace blinked a few times, her vision clearing up and listened to JoJo answer the phone. At least she hadn't been lying about a home phone. Maybe things weren't as dire as Grace thought they were. Maybe they were just going to let her call and then let her go. They could have just been having some kind of lovers spat in the other room.

Grace smirked again. She knew better, but her head was trying to calm her down.

JoJo and the guy she called Rick came out of the room. Grace sat up straight and noticed the no nonsense looks on their faces. JoJo pulled a seat and faced her.

"A situation has come up, so I don't have any time to talk a load of bullshit or to hear any back. I know who you are. I know who your father is. And I'm pretty sure you've got enough brains in your head to have figured that out already."

"Wouldn't take a genius. What do you want?"

"I want to know why you didn't walk out that door once you realized I brought you here on purpose."

"Ha. Is that all? Because my father's an asshole. I wouldn't have been looking to call him if I didn't have any other option. Why not sit in a stranger's living room and see what happens?"

"What happened?"

"Nothing I can't handle."

"I said no time for bullshit. What happened?"

"Dad's right hand man, a guy named Cuba, grabbed me from my yacht and tried to hold me captive. Probably to put some leverage on my father for the ..."

"Treasure."

"Oh, you know about that. Great. Show my dad a pair of tits and he'll spill all the secrets. Anyway, I got away and here I am. No better or worse for it."

"Do you want to go back to your father?"

"Not if you have a better idea. This is supposed to be a vacation for me, after all."

"Do you trust me?"

"No, not at all. But I don't trust anyone at this point."

"Good enough." JoJo stood up and gestured for Grace to get up. "Let's go."

Rick opened the door, first one out, still not saying a word to Grace.

"Where are we going?"

"Down to the docks to meet a friend of ours. I spent some time with your father, got to know him. He is a scumbag. But he's a scumbag with a map to a shit ton of gold. Or, at least he was."

"You stole the map?" Grace asked as they left the apartment.

"Yes. Then some little shit stole it from me."

"Where's this little shit now?"

"On board the boat of a Captain and diver I brought on to help us get to the loot. He says that he went out to check to make sure that the map was right, to see if there really was some sort of wreck. My thoughts? He went out to see if he could get it alone and it turned out he needed people. But I'll deal with him later. Right now, we get down there and we go to the site."

"Why the rush?"

"Because apparently the little shit is screaming bloody murder and Alberto doesn't want to hit him in the head again. Felt bad the first time he did it."

"And you need me because?"

JoJo stopped for a moment, looking around to see if anyone was following them.

"Because I think you left out a bit from that story you told. I think this Cuba guy took you because you know more about the situation than you're letting on. Because you know exactly where it is and what's under there. Knowledge is power, right?"

JoJo started walking again. Grace shrugged and followed.

If knowledge was power, how come so many stupid people had most of the power?

THIRTY-TWO

Maria was surprised to get the phone call from Raul, who she'd thought had finally lost his mind and was in the wind, building a hit squad to come for her. She knew it was only a matter of time.

"Where are you?" Maria asked Raul.

"I am at the northern villa and I have a prize with me, of sorts," Raul said. Maria could hear his excitement over the phone. "A rogue DEA agent who says he can help us locate the treasure and he only wants his fair share."

Maria laughed. How many people were trying for this supposedly secret treasure? She wondered if Ernie had brought this agent in. "What's his name?"

"Baker Cioffi. I've had him run and he does check out. He's a legit agent, but get this... he is on vacation right now. Not working in Mexico. He has to know about this from Patek, but I'm waiting on your order to torture the information from him or not."

"Hold." Maria walked into the other room, where Ernie was lying on the bed with an empty beer bottle balanced on his sizable belly. "Do you know a DEA Agent Cioffi? Baker is his first name."

Ernie frowned. "No. Doesn't ring a bell. Should I know him?"

"Have you had DEA agents following you?"

Ernie smiled. "Only for the last ten years or so. They know I'm doing something illegal all the time but they can never figure it out. Why?"

"Because it looks like this agent knows about the shipwreck and the treasure, and he's come down to Mexico on his own to worm his way into the search," Maria said.

She sighed and put the phone back to her ear. "You heard all of that? Don't do anything with him yet. No, better to bring him back here so we can put him and Ernie together and see if they actually know each other. If Patek has brought in the United States government, this could be really bad. Be here within the hour."

Maria needed to consolidate everyone right now and figure out the next move.

She turned back to Ernie, who was smiling as he shook the empty beer bottle in her direction, as if she was a waitress.

"What's the chance I get another cold one, pretty senorita?"

Maria smiled even though she wanted to kick the man in his crotch. "That depends... what are you not telling me?"

"About what?" Ernie tried to sit up in bed but failed, rolling back and forth like an overturned turtle. "I told you everything I know. I promise."

Maria shrugged. "Then you are useless to me, right?" She really wanted to kill him but decided to hold for at least a bit longer, especially with this DEA agent about to arrive at the villa.

Without another word she left the room, locking the door behind her. The fat man could go without more alcohol for another hour. She wasn't going to wait on him anymore, either. He'd eat when everyone else was going to eat. No more snacks. No more special treatment.

Not until he tells us where the damn treasure really is, Maria thought.

She made sure a few men loyal to her were at her side at all times now, because this could still be a trick from Raul. There might not be a DEA agent. Even if there was, it might be a good distraction.

Maria sighed as she poured herself a generous helping of tequila in the kitchen.

Am I being paranoid? No, I'm being smart. Raul will eventually make his move but it would be smarter for him if he waited until I helped him to retrieve the valuables, she thought.

The tequila went down smoothly but she didn't refill her glass. She needed to keep her wits. Needed to be sure Raul wasn't going to make his move sooner than later.

Maria decided once the treasure was on deck of whatever boat they used, she'd have one of her men put a bullet in Raul's head and pitch him overboard. See if his loyal crew were going to shoot it out or likely change sides and think they'd get part of the treasure.

In actuality, they'd all be separated and tortured for information, to see how deep the conspiracy went. Did Raul have other, more powerful, backers for his attempt to usurp her crown?

Maria didn't meet Raul's entourage when he arrived forty minutes later, preferring the safety of the balcony above the parking area. She'd positioned three of her men with rifles in the event Raul tried to play dirty.

The man Raul had with him definitely looked like an American government agent.

Perhaps this isn't a distraction or a bluff, Maria thought.

She met Raul and his prisoner in the side meeting room, where everyone sat and smiled at one another.

"I am Maria and I run this area for the cartel, in case you had no clue who I was," Maria said, pointedly staring at Raul as she told the DEA agent who she was. As if the man didn't already know.

"As I was telling your man here–"

Maria put up a hand. "I will ask the questions and you will answer them. This conversation isn't going to be run by you, Mister Agent Man. Got it?"

Baker nodded.

"How do you know about the treasure?" Maria asked. She tried not to smile as she noticed how uncomfortable Raul was. He'd brought the agent here, thinking he'd be doing the questioning.

Maria had made sure to time this next part and now she did smile as Ernie Patek was led inside the meeting room, looking tired and slobbish.

"Sit next to your friend from the United States," Maria said to Ernie.

Ernie sat down next to Baker, but she could see the two men didn't know one another personally. Maybe Baker knew Ernie since the DEA would be tracking the man.

Baker looked like he wanted to continue his speech, but Maria wasn't going to let him.

"You walk into my life and think you can make demands about a treasure that isn't yours, Mister Agent Man," Maria said. She pointed at Ernie. "This fool had a map of the location but he lost it because a woman actually paid attention to him. Now we're no closer than we ever were. So... do you see why you showing up, in the midst of all of this, might seem... hmm... foolish?"

Baker was sweating. "I can see it from that point of view, but I've been doing my homework. My research on all of this, and I think I can add value."

"And how would you be able to do that?" Raul asked.

Maria gave Raul a dirty look. He was supposed to sit and shut his mouth while she was in charge.

Another strike against him, she thought. "Answer the question."

Baker smiled. "The people who have the map will hire a boat captain. They'll go to the spot and retrieve whatever is down there. Don't you see? Let them do all of the work and then we swoop in and take it. Very simple."

Maria shrugged. It was what she'd been thinking, as long as they figured out who this other group was and how connected they actually were. "And how do you play into all of this? By saying something that we were all thinking? Your plan isn't unique or brilliant or something I never thought of."

"No, but I can help us get some of the treasure smuggled into the United States and sold for better than pennies on the dollar, which is what you'd get in South America," Baker said.

"Interesting," Maria said. She looked at Raul. "They both get to live another day. Put them in separate, secure rooms. I will assign several men to the docks to see if there is anything happening already."

Maria knew she'd need to pick men loyal to her, so that Raul couldn't double-cross her.

She dismissed everyone and went back to the kitchen to pour herself another tequila.

THIRTY-THREE

They were one-hundred feet out from the dock before Rick let out a deep breath. The walk to the boat was more stressful than he had thought, and he'd been expecting it to be anxiety-ridden. Not only did he have to worry about the cartel looking for JoJo, but now he had to look out for some crazed rogue muscle from fat Ernie Patek's crew named Cuba.

The FBI rarely operated outside U.S. borders, so Rick had never had a chance to go to Cuba. But he'd heard stories from some of his CIA friends, and the criminal element there was possibly more brutal than the Mexican cartel.

Rick didn't think he was making too much of a leap guessing this guy was from Cuba. It was his name, after all. Who would name their kid Cuba unless they were Cuban.

Snap out of it, Rick thought as he turned to make sure JoJo and Grace were still behind him.

Rick had found himself getting too easily distracted from what needed to be done. That itch to get high was always with him, and combined with his constant worry about having to protect JoJo he was not on top of the game like he should be.

But the walk to Alberto's boat had been mostly uneventful. There was some sort of party going on at the docks and bar.

Lots of grilles, loud music, and drinks floating around as they had snaked their way to the boat.

One partier had slammed into him so hard, Rick was about to knock him out before the man began apologizing loudly and profusely in Spanish, obviously obliterated.

Now, as the boat made its way further from shore, Rick tried to concentrate on the steady rhythm of the engine and the swells to keep his mind off just what he wouldn't give to shoot up one more time.

JoJo had told Alberto to untie Nacho once they were far enough away from land, and now the kid was stomping up and down the boat yelling so fast, Rick could barely make out what he was saying. He knew most of it included some pretty inventive cursing.

Grace sat on one of the padded benches, smirking at the scene. JoJo stood between the kid and Alberto, pushing Nacho away each time he came close to Alberto. If Rick was in the mood, he would have been laughing at the situation. As it was, it took all his energy to get in the mindset for this treasure.

Alberto had said that he wasn't sure if their efforts would start today or not. He hadn't dove when he came to check out the wreck site, and he couldn't see much from above water besides just a vague outline of it. He had decided not to dive it and wait for JoJo and Rick to join him.

Rick didn't know if he could get in the water. Not the way he was feeling. Besides, someone would have to watch Nacho, and he didn't trust Grace at all. She'd probably steal the boat and leave them all stranded.

Rick, JoJo, and Alberto had discussed it, and it was decided that Alberto and JoJo would make the initial dive, just to check out the situation and assess what they would need to raise up whatever they could salvage.

Rick had figured most would be able to be vacuumed up, an easier task then loading everything onto netting and winching it up to the surface.

That was, if the situation at the bottom allowed for the hose to be used without it getting caught up or torn in the wreckage.

Rick turned his back to the ocean and sat across from Grace. JoJo had wanted to bring her, but he still wasn't sure exactly why. She mentioned that Grace may have some information that would help them either during the salvage or after, maybe the best way to avoid running into Patek's men.

Rick looked at Grace as she stared, amused at Nacho's antics.

He had known JoJo for a long time. They'd gone through a hell of a situation before they deported themselves to Mexico under assumed names. JoJo didn't give a damn about most people. Only a handful of people could call her and have her on the next plane to wherever they were. But Rick knew one thing: she'd made her own way in the world since a young adult, never working a normal job, and conning her way around the country.

She was a free spirit and, looking at Grace, Rick saw the same thing.

Why did JoJo really want to bring her along? Probably because Grace reminded her of herself when she was younger. Maybe she felt some kind of motherly protectiveness over this person they'd only met a couple hours ago.

The boat slowed down and came to a stop. Nacho had finally exhausted himself and was sitting next to Rick.

"Over here," Alberto said. JoJo followed him to the side of the boat and they both looked down.

"That's definitely a wreck. The map was spot on," JoJo said.

"I'll drop anchor. Let's suit up and get down there," Alberto said.

Rick looked at Nacho, who may have calmed down but still looked like a pissed off little tiger. Rick shrugged and looked at Grace, who had a confused look on her face.

"What's wrong?" Rick asked.

"Why are we stopping? I thought we were going to the wreck," Grace said.

"Yeah, apparently we're here."

Grace shook her head. "No, this is wrong. Nate and I were on top of the damn thing." She pointed at a peak of land in the distance. "You definitely couldn't see that. Also, the water wasn't this shallow."

"What are you saying? The map is wrong?" JoJo asked, overhearing their conversation.

"It must be. Let me see it." JoJo handed it over to Grace, who took a few moments to look it over. "No. I don't know what this is, but it's definitely not a map to where the wreck is."

Alberto let out a growl and grabbed Nacho by the shirt, twisted and threw the kid airborne. Nacho landed in the water with a yelp.

"You gave me a fake map, you little shit," Alberto said.

"No, I took it off Miss JoJo. I saw her take it off the fat man. It's real, I swear. Get me out of here, please."

Rick laughed at Nacho's face. The kid was petrified of being in the water and he treaded water violently begging for Alberto to lift him out.

"Bullshit. You've always been a con artist. I just don't know what your point was of trying to bring me out here with a fake map."

"It's not fake, I swear. Ah! Something touched my foot. I'm going to get eaten out here. Please."

JoJo reached over and lifted Nacho out of the water, tossing him to the boat's floor like she'd caught him on a fishing pole.

"He's right," Grace said. "This is the same map my father had. I've seen it enough times to know the creases in it. But why would it bring us out here? Out to an actual wreck but not the one anybody is looking for?"

"Did your father think the map was to the actual treasure, or was he using it as a decoy?"

"No, he really thought this was it. But …"

"But what?" Rick asked.

"But there were coordinates in the yacht that brought us to the actual wreck. Why would he put the correct coordinates in but still think this map led to the same place?"

"None of this is making sense," JoJo said, pacing the boat. "Ernie absolutely thought that map brought us to the treasure. Unless someone else programmed the yacht."

"Like who?" Alberto said.

"Cuba," Grace said and stood up.

"That actually makes sense," JoJo said.

"No. Cuba," Grace said and pointed behind them.

A boat was at the horizon and approaching fast. They weren't heading in their direction by coincidence.

"How the hell was someone able to find–" Rick began to say and stopped. He thought back to the walk to the boat and the drunk guy who bumped into him. Bumped into him a little too hard.

Rick began searching his pockets and groaned as he felt something small, about the size of an M&M. He pulled out the tracking device and tossed it into the water.

"You guys may want to pull anchor and gun it. Unless you want Cuba to kill all of you," Grace said and sat down, her face blank.

THIRTY-FOUR

Raul knew the call had come after the man had called someone else first. That was how it worked: the highest bidder got the first call. It didn't matter, because they might be behind but they'd soon catch up.

Again, Raul knew they didn't need to be the first to the shipwreck, just the first to it when the treasure was pulled from the ocean floor.

Maria was also going, which he knew was because she didn't trust him. That was fine with Raul, because he would do the same thing in her position.

No one was left behind at the villa, including their two prisoners.

"Three small boats," Maria had shouted as they piled into their SUVs.

Raul was glad he wasn't driving with her, but knew she'd want him close when they got to the docks. In his vehicle were men loyal to him, but he wasn't going to say a word in fear she'd bugged all of the vehicles.

They drove toward the docks, the drivers beeping their horns and flashing their lights so people would get out of the way.

As if the townsfolk had no idea who was barreling down the dusty streets.

When they arrived at the docks, Maria joined Raul. "Give me whatever information you heard."

"Alberto went out with a few people. Definitely the woman who stole the map. Perhaps Grace, Ernie's daughter. A gringo and one of the street urchins." Raul knew Maria was likely annoyed he'd received the call and not her, but he was the one who'd made the connections in town. He'd had to do the grunt work when they'd first arrived and set up his network, not her.

Maria was too busy suntanning and drinking to worry about what was actually happening and the reason they were here in the first place. For her it was all about the look, the showiness of being important.

Not the actual grunt work that needed to be done, which was what Raul had to always do. His hands were always dirty, not hers. He swore, when he became the de facto leader, his hands would still get dirty and he'd put in the actual work.

Raul was now the one shouting orders to the men to collect three fast boats and load them up quickly. He knew every man was armed with a rifle and a sidearm, and he hoped there would be shooting today. He'd grown so tired of playing politics all the time and standing by idly while Maria talked your ear off about the ways things needed to be.

He preferred the way things used to be, thank you very much.

Back when he was a boy, his father and uncles had run a successful business or two within the cartel, producing so much cash they couldn't keep it all safely. With the prostitution, drugs and weapons running they were a big deal.

Until people like Maria, who worried about their image more than the moneymakers, who bribed people for their own ego instead of doing it because it truly helped the cartel and increased their network, came to power.

Now he had to stand and be counted, just another small cog in the wheel of this new cartel.

Maria was not underground. She was not hiding from the spotlight. She wanted to grace the covers of magazines, to have her picture in the papers.

This new cartel wasn't going to work, and the sooner Raul could drag it back underground the better. Hadn't she learned from the past? Escobar and El Chapo and all the rest. They'd become bigger than the cartel, known and interesting. They were targets and the reason blood had been spilled on the cartel side in gallons.

Maria and Raul were on the same boat together, which was fine with him. Better to hear her orders first-hand instead of being passed along.

"What do you think we should do?" Maria asked Raul, surprising him.

"I think we keep our distance. Only one boat gets close enough to see what is happening with binoculars. We don't need to kill anyone, we need them to find the shipwreck and the treasure. Once they pull the wealth from the ocean we can surround them and take it for our own," Raul said.

Maria nodded slowly, as if what he'd said was so over the top and unexpected.

Raul wanted to scream. What plan had been formulated in her head? Was she thinking about attacking whoever was out there and forcing them to get the treasure, or did she think there were divers among her crew? Because Raul already knew there weren't.

He'd taken diving lessons as a teenager and he loved it, but it wasn't a skill too many people knew he possessed. Like most things, he kept it to himself.

You never knew when you'd need to use a particular skill or when it was going to be called upon. Better to surprise the people around you than for them to rely on you using it for their own gain.

"Good plan," Maria said. "We will go ahead and leave the other boats behind, within calling distance."

Raul nodded, knowing she'd take the praise if this worked out and he'd take the heat if it did not. No matter. As long as he got his hands on some gold or silver he'd be fine.

It would eventually lead to his taking over the cartel.

When they got nearly within sight of the boat, based on the information from the person who'd watched them leave and had tagged one of the passengers, Raul ordered the other two boats to stop and anchor. They'd be needed soon enough, so this wasn't a relaxing day in the sun for the crews.

"Forward," Raul shouted to the captain of the boat.

Maria had unbuttoned her top, exposing a lot of cleavage. Raul tried not to look, thinking she was trying to distract him.

It was working and Raul finally moved his seat behind her, shaking his head.

"Is there something the matter?" Maria asked with a grin, turning around to face Raul.

"No, ma'am. Waiting to see what happens next." Raul made sure to keep his eyes on the horizon as they sped toward it. He wanted nothing to do with Maria or her games.

All he wanted was to see her beg for her life before he ended it. All he needed was the power so close he could almost touch it.

Raul knew there would be bloodshed. A small, short civil war in the cartel, before things would settle down. Because whether you loved or hated whoever was in charge, the promise of money and power could cure any ill will toward them.

"I see a ship up ahead," a man shouted. He had binoculars pressed to his face. "I think it is them, and they might be anchored."

"Excellent," Maria said and stood up, right in front of Raul.

It took him an extra few seconds to take his eyes from her taut ass and look to see where this boat was in the distance.

THIRTY-FIVE

JoJo got Grace and Nacho down the steps and out of sight. The less people visible, the better. Especially if this Cuba guy was on the boat. Grace could pull the wool over most people's eyes, but she wasn't able to hide the look of fear on her face when she mentioned him.

Even though Grace had told them to take off, Alberto recognized the type of boat coming their way. He told JoJo there was no point in trying to out-race it. The engine on the approaching boat made his look like a Tonka toy.

JoJo ran through their options. If this was the cartel approaching, she could try handing over the fake map. Point to the wreck below them. That should be convincing enough. Probably not enough to stop them from putting bullets in all of their heads, but maybe enough to buy more time.

If it was Cuba, the map wouldn't hold up. Ernie Patek's right-hand-man would have known it was fake from the beginning. No, Cuba wasn't coming for the treasure. He knew where that was. He was coming for Grace. If he was anything like the other macho men JoJo had run into during her life, Grace's ballsy escape was an embarrassment to him. He would have lost face in front of his men, and people like Cuba don't stand for that.

"Either way, we're probably all fucked," JoJo said.

"More than you know," Rick said behind her.

JoJo turned and he handed her the binoculars he had been looking through. She scanned the area he was facing and stopped on another boat, much further out. Someone stood on that boat looking right back with another set of binoculars. Also, he and the other people were all strapped with some nasty looking automatics.

"Those are Raul's men," Alberto said, wiping his hands with a rag.

"How can you tell?"

"Who else would be out here? This man Cuba has slowed down. Probably spotted the other boats."

"So our choices are we wait for the cartel to kill us, or we wait for some rogue guy from Patek's crew to kill us," Rick said.

"Or we sit here and just get caught in the crossfire between the two of them. Anyone want to place bets on who gets shot by who?" JoJo asked.

Alberto leaned over and dipped his hands in the water, shaking them briskly before continuing to wipe them with a towel.

JoJo looked at his hands and gave Alberto a strange look.

"What were you doing?"

"Rick, can you look inside the bench over there and let me know how many minis I have?"

Rick opened the top or the bench. He counted half a dozen miniature oxygen tanks. He also spotted an unopened bag of Doritos, which he immediately grabbed.

"Six," Rick said with a mouthful of chips.

"That will work. JoJo, go downstairs and give Nacho and the woman a tank each. Grab one for yourself. Rick, raise the anchor. I should have just enough left to get this thing turned sideways in both boats' direction."

"Just enough what?" Rick asked.

"Oil." Alberto tossed the soiled rag on the floor of the boat. That's when JoJo noticed the smell in the air and realized what Alberto was doing.

"Shit," JoJo said, and grabbed three tanks and went down the stairs.

She found Grace and Nacho sitting on the bed saying nothing to each other. Nacho was shivering a little, but his clothes had started to dry. Too bad that wasn't going to last long.

She handed them both a tank.

"You know how to use these?"

Grace nodded. The way Nacho stared at it, JoJo didn't need him to answer. She spent as little time as possible showing him the basics. She didn't know how fast they would need to get in the water, but JoJo was sure Alberto wasn't going to waste any time.

Nacho looked petrified at the concept. JoJo told him some bullshit about sharks not coming into this part of the ocean because they didn't like the temperature. He seemed to calm down a little, but not by much.

JoJo hadn't brought up that the cartel was also now in the picture. She didn't want to make the anxiety worse.

"Get by the stairs and wait there until I tell you to come up. When I do, we're going straight off the boat. We… shit. Hold on."

JoJo went up top. Rick and Alberto had maneuvered the boat so the port side was facing the boats. It smelled strongly of engine oil and gasoline. She could see some of the fumes wavering in the air.

"I need face masks now."

"In the back," Alberto said.

JoJo grabbed two masks and gave them to Grace and Nacho.

"Put these on now. When I tell you to come up, you go straight in the water. Alberto and Rick will already be in there. Just stick close to them. If you need it, they'll be there to help. I'll be right behind you."

"What's happening?" Grace asked.

"A little more problems than we expected. But we'll be fine."

JoJo went up to the deck again. Rick was standing there looking nervous, but ready to jump. Alberto had a mix of sadness and anger in his face.

"How far do you think we can get before this goes up?" JoJo asked.

"Hopefully far enough that we don't get killed. By the cartel? Sure. That happens all the time. Getting killed by a boat you exploded? That's just stupid."

Alberto didn't give a warning. He flipped off the boats in the distance and lit the trail of oil and gas. JoJo didn't want to think about the environmental damage they were about to cause.

"Go. Go." Alberto turned as the port side of the boat lit up with flames, blocking Cuba and the cartel's view of the deck. Then, without waiting for anyone else, he leapt into the water.

Rick followed him.

"Up now, guys. Come on." JoJo waited for Grace and Nacho to get topside.

Grace went right into the water. Nacho stopped, but JoJo was expecting that and, for the second time today, Nacho got tossed into the water.

JoJo jumped just as she saw the flames getting closer to the back of the boat. They'd have less time than Alberto was probably expecting.

She had just made it in when the first bullet pinged off the boat.

JoJo went under and saw Rick had Nacho by the back of his shirt, keeping the kid from surfacing. At least Nacho had kept hold of his tank.

Alberto pointed the direction they should head in and JoJo gave a thumbs up.

The five of them swam as fast as they could as it began to rain bullets around them.

Then, a bright light and a strange underwater sound, and they were all hit by the shockwave.

The boat had blown.

THIRTY-SIX

Maria had to smile or she thought she'd cry. Of course, she'd never show emotion in front of Raul and the men on the boat with her. She figured out what they were doing a second before she saw the flames.

She also knew they weren't going to kill themselves, so they had a plan B, which was likely going underwater.

"Fire at the boat and the surrounding water if you have a high-powered rifle," Maria shouted.

Several gunshots immediately ran out, men who wanted nothing more than to kill.

Raul had his arms folded across his chest and was staring out at the boat as it began to burn, the wind helping it.

"Why aren't you also shooting?" Maria asked Raul. It was more to gauge his thoughts than to bust his balls. She knew he had an idea or two in his pretty little head. As much as she worried he would try to take over from her, she knew he was a bold strategist and had risen in the ranks because he usually did all the right things.

"I don't want to kill a dolphin accidentally." Raul turned away from Maria and went to where his men were standing and shooting.

Maria smiled. He definitely had something up his sleeve and she knew he'd put it into motion soon enough. She hoped it wasn't going to be at an inopportune time for her.

"What about the other boat, Raul?" Maria asked as she approached him. She needed him to focus on the outward threats right now and not worry about putting into motion whatever his plan was for her.

Raul turned and stared at the other boat in the distance, too far for them to see who it was. "DEA, perhaps? Another cartel trying to sneak into our territory? Maybe another local with dreams of riches? It could be anyone."

"We'll need to deal with them at some point, too," Maria said. "They're too close to the burning boat for us to approach safely without getting into a gunfight."

Raul turned to her and shrugged. "If they want a gunfight, we are more than prepared."

"Very true," Maria said. "Have our other two boats come up and join us. Head slowly toward the burning boat and watch the water. I'm sure they went into the water. They'll need to pass us to get back to land, so they should be easy enough to see and kill."

As the boat began to move closer to the burning boat Maria took a deep breath. Killing whoever survived the explosion would be easy enough, but then would it become a dead end to find the treasure? She was sure Ernie Patek knew nothing. The DEA agent knew even less, she was sure.

Maria turned to both men, tied together and seated in the middle of the boat.

"Can you see? Need anything?" Maria asked.

Ernie smiled. "A beer would be nice. Also, a hat. My head is on fire."

Maria pointed across the water. "Imagine how hot it is on that boat, right?"

Ernie laughed uneasily. Maria noticed the DEA agent was tight-lipped and watching in silence.

"Who do you think was on that boat, and how close do you think they were to the shipwreck?" Maria asked Ernie, bending down in front of him and giving the fat man a good shot of her crotch and her chest.

Ernie licked his lips. *So stupid*, she thought. "Tell me who else is in play."

"It could be anyone," Ernie said. His eyes were glued on Maria, shifting up and down. "Maybe the bitch that stole the map."

Maria stood. She felt like she was wasting time.

The boat made a noise like thunder on the ocean, deep and booming, before it slipped underwater and was gone. Only a small smoke trail from floating bits and pieces marked where it had been a second ago.

Maria noticed the other boat was still nearby but as soon as her other two boats approached from behind, the other boat turned and fled.

Good. I don't need another complication right now, Maria thought.

Raul's men had stopped firing, all bent over the rail now and looking for anyone in the water.

Maria groaned to herself. She'd thought of them as Raul's men, which was not a good thing. As soon as she returned to the villa she'd make a call and have a dozen men loyal to her come over from Mexico City and even the odds in her favor.

"I think we toss one of these two overboard with a bullet in their head to attract the sharks and let whoever was on that boat know we're coming," Raul said quietly. He pulled his weapon and put the muzzle to the DEA agent's temple.

As much as Maria wanted to nod and let him do it, she knew this was likely part of his powerplay. He'd start making demands and if she went along with it, that might show everyone he was in charge.

"No. We still need them and their information," Maria said and turned away, showing Raul she wasn't worried he'd go against her. She also casually slipped a hand near her own weapon, because if she heard a shot she'd need to return her own.

We're so close right now. If Raul took this moment to try to usurp her power, it would only complicate things, Maria thought.

If Raul was smart, Maria knew he'd wait until the treasure was in their hands and being counted. Then the real fireworks would start.

"Have all three boats do a grid pattern and find whoever is still in the water," Maria said. "I want them found. Not killed, either. We need some answers first." She glanced at Raul. "And then, and only then, will I allow you to kill them."

If I don't kill you first, Maria thought.

Raul stared at her a few seconds too long before nodding his head and giving orders to not only the men on their boat but radioed to the other boats to spread out and search.

Maria did her own glance at Ernie and Baker, wondering how they played into all of this and what she'd need to do with them in the end. They weren't going to survive this no matter what, but she hoped to at least get some important information out of the two of them.

A DEA agent always had something for her to use, so she had no worries he'd beg for his life and give up locations and secrets in order to save his own skin.

Ernie Patek was the wild card, because he was selfish and only in this for himself. She doubted he had any real information she could use in the future, but he had a lot of good underworld contacts she could use.

Maybe these two men would get a slight reprieve before they were killed, just long enough to use and then toss out with the rest of the trash.

Raul was staring at her, but when Maria looked at him, he turned away.

Yes, it would be good to take out all of the trash, Maria thought.

THIRTY-SEVEN

There was no reason to head toward the mainland unless they all wanted to be turned into shark chum. Alberto, not in the mood to be riddled with bullets, brought them further out to sea.

Rick signaled him, asking why they were going out further. Alberto motioned back to trust him and kept the lead as the others swam behind him.

Considering the amount of times he and Rick had sat at the bar going beer for beer until they stumbled home, Alberto figured Rick would have more faith in him. But gringos, by nature, seemed to be cautious at best, untrusting at worst.

Luckily they had been far enough away from the boat when it exploded that the shockwave only gave them a rough shove rather than shattering a few bones. Grace's tank had dropped and JoJo was sharing hers. They took turns pulling air and holding it. JoJo could go a couple minutes before needing the tank back, which didn't surprise Alberto. He knew she was experienced. Grace, however, seemed to be able to keep pace with JoJo, if not surpass her in breath holding.

Alberto couldn't help but watch her underwater, moving as if she belonged there. The girl definitely knew the water and her motions and actions made him wonder what the real reason Cuba was so hot to get her back.

He heard the boats in the distance, the sound of the motors getting louder then fading away, then growing again. They were searching for them. Making a grid, Alberto figured from the pattern of the rising and fading.

Knowing more than most about how a grid search worked, he knew they'd initially keep closer to land, but eventually start making their way further out even though that would require much more mass to cover.

Alberto wasn't worried. They'd get to where he was bringing them long before the boats would sail overhead. And at least the bullets had stopped piercing the water around them, leaving long strips of white water trailing around like holiday streamers.

Alberto saw it in the distance. He turned and pointed in the direction of the underwater cave. He noticed Rick holding Nacho's tank against his mouth. A line of pink trailed into the distance behind the kid. Rick was struggling.

Alberto swam to the other side of the kid and put his hand under his arm. The cave wasn't too much further away, but the burden of carrying dead weight was quickly gassing him out.

They made their way into the cave and the bright sunlight that had been filtering through the water was left behind. Alberto motioned for them to stop while there was still enough light to see.

He reached down and unclipped the underwater flashlight he'd attached to his shorts before abandoning ship. It took a couple hits to the side, but the light came on, although a little dim for his liking.

How many times have I said I'm going to start checking safety equipment daily? Alberto thought.

He led them through the cave system, stalactites reaching down from the ceiling to try to attack them. At a curve in the cave, he flipped off the flashlight to confirm he'd gone the right way.

Just above and ahead of them, a dull blue light illuminated the water. Alberto pointed and they made their way up, heads coming out of the water into an underground grotto.

JoJo, who had been holding her breath during the last leg, inhaled sharply.

"Quick, get him on the ledge," Rick said.

Alberto and Rick lifted Nacho out of the water onto the slick rocky ledge. It was an outgrowth just large enough for maybe three people. Two would have to remain in the water and hold on to the edge.

JoJo and Grace both asked what happened at the same time. Neither had apparently noticed the leaking wound as they made their way to their current hideout.

Rick lifted up Nacho's shirt and winced. Blood was seeping out of the bullet wound in his abdomen. Rick turned him on his side and Nacho let out a meek cry. He was conscious but seemed to not know where he was.

There was no exit wound, which meant the bullet was somewhere inside him. Either lodged in bone or organ. Neither was a good situation.

"He's not bleeding too bad. I can keep pressure on it. Wrap my shirt around it or something," Grace said.

"Look at the blood. It's almost black. The bullet probably perforated his liver, possibly cutting through his bowel also."

"So we get him help. There's light in here which means there has to be a way out."

"If his bowels are leaking shit into his abdominal cavity, and his liver is shredded, he may not make it long enough for any real help," Rick said. He took Nacho's shirt off, to more groans of pain, rolled it up, and put it under Nacho's head.

"We can't just give up. He can make it. I know he can." Grace pulled herself up onto the ledge, almost knocking Alberto back into the water.

JoJo reached up and put a hand on Grace's knee. Grace looked at her, her eyes filled with desperation to do something, anything, to get the kid out and to help. JoJo just shook her head, saying nothing.

Alberto wanted to say something to put everyone at ease, but he didn't trust his voice to not crack. He'd seen many bullet wounds in his life, and he knew when one was beyond help.

Nacho began to groan louder, the sound of his agony bouncing off the small grotto walls. He was starting to come out of shock and would soon be in an immense amount of pain.

Rick winced and felt tears hover in his eyes, enough to blur his vision. He blinked and quickly wiped away the tears.

Nacho began moving, trying to sit up, and the groans turned to screams.

"Do something. We have to do something, please. Let me find the way out. I can bring someone back here," Grace pleaded, covering her ears.

Rick looked down at JoJo, floating in the water. She stared back at him.

Rick sighed and pulled out a small waterproof dive bag that he'd stuffed his items in before they all went in the water. He pulled out a pocket knife and a black balloon a little smaller than a marble.

He punched a hole in it with the knife and a little bit of brown powder spilled out onto his hand. He scooped a very small amount onto the tip of the knife and tossed the rest aside.

After a little bit of maneuvering and coaxing, he was able to get Nacho to sniff the powder. The kid wretched and threw up a little, but then his screaming slowly stopped and he laid back down, staring at the mossy ceiling.

"I didn't use any. I just had it because–" Rick began to explain to JoJo.

"Stop. We will talk about this later. But right now your mistake is giving the kid some relief, so I'll choose to focus on that for now." JoJo then turned and watched Nacho, refusing to look at Rick.

"Mama," Nacho said.

Rick ran his hand through the kid's hair, trying to soothe him. "It's ok. We're here."

"No. Take care of Mama. Money under board in my room by heater. She gets my cut of the treasure."

"Nacho, there's no reason to talk–"

"I told you, stupid gringo, I don't like that name." He coughed and a string of blood landed on his chin.

Rick nodded. "Ok, Ignacio. Where is your mama? I'll make sure she's taken care of."

Nacho laughed, even though it obviously hurt him. "Don't worry. She'll find you. And if she doesn't kill all of you, then you can give her my cut."

"We need to get out of here soon," Alberto said. "It's low tide now, but high tide will be coming soon and this whole place will flood.

Rick agreed and went to pick up Nacho, but his body was limp. He checked his pulse and put a hand under his nose. No sign of life. He picked up the body and told Alberto to lead the way.

Not only did they have to worry about the cartel and Cuba, but now they would have to find a way to carry a dead body somewhere safe without anybody noticing.

Alberto saw the hatred in Rick's face and knew what he was thinking. He'd worry about trying to talk Rick out of going after the cartel later. For now, he needed to focus on getting them out of there. And avoiding Nacho's mother. She would find out about her son sooner than later. People had a way of finding out secrets around town.

There was nothing more dangerous than a grieving Mexican mother.

THIRTY-EIGHT

Cuba was beyond frustrated. There were too many boats in his line of vision and who knew if there were more just over the horizon.

"What should we do, boss?"

Cuba didn't really know. He wanted to make sure Grace was safe. He wondered why. Was it because she was his flesh and blood, or because she was a useful pawn against Ernie Patek?

His thoughts had always been strange when it came to Grace. He tried to be hands-off and keep his distance, but the woman had been a nightmare when she was in her teenage years. Ernie never paid proper attention to her, never gave her life skills she would need later in life, and Grace had no limit to what she could or couldn't do.

All the money in the world didn't mean you were a good parent. It usually meant, like in the case of the Patek family, you threw hundred dollar bills at every problem and moved on.

When Grace was sixteen she'd crashed a 2010 Jaguar XF her father had bought only a week before for over a hundred grand with every bell and whistle imaginable. She'd been drunk, her and her girlfriends drinking MD 20/20 and wanting to stop at a Taco Bell for food to soak up the alcohol. Instead, she'd hit the gas instead of the brake and taken out the drive thru order display.

And what had happened to Grace? Nothing. Ernie paid for the damages, had his gauntlet of lawyers make sure no charges were ever near his daughter, and made a sizable donation to a lot of people to turn the other way.

Cuba knew it didn't help Grace grow as a person. It let her know she could do anything she wanted and there were never going to be any repercussions. Never going to be an arrest or a slap on the wrist. Her life was literally whatever she made it.

In quieter moments Cuba would talk to her, letting her know the real world didn't work like her mother and father had rolled out the red carpet for her, and he guessed some of what he said actually stuck.

Grace wasn't a mean person. She never took advantage of anyone and never pushed the envelope too much. She was happy to get drunk, get a tan and order more clothes than she could possibly wear.

He liked that she was also generous to her friends and loyal, too. On more than one occasion Grace would help out people in need and had started doing more charity work, even if most of it was because her father got her involved thanks to some of the work her mother had done before her death.

Cuba sighed, thinking of the magical nights he'd had with Grace's mother. He knew the one that led to conceiving Grace, too, and it was a secret, fond memory.

"Boss... some of these boats are getting too close for comfort."

He had to make a decision. When the boat had blown up he'd been overcome with fear Grace was gone, but once he'd settled down he knew it was impossible. It was nothing more than an old captain's trick to get away from pursuit you could never outrun.

The cartel boats, and he knew that was what was circling them, were too fast for an old fishing boat.

Grace is fine. She's alive and right now swimming underneath this boat to safety, Cuba thought. It's what he needed to believe.

"Turn back. No use in getting into a gunfight on the open seas," Cuba shouted with a smile. He needed to focus and make sure his men were safe and there'd be another day to fight in their future.

While he trusted the men he had under him, he didn't have one standout, which bothered him. He hardly ever called them by name or even thought of them as anything other than a random henchman under his payroll. They all looked and acted the same. All ex-military, with military haircuts, huge biceps and shaded sunglasses.

Like cartoon characters. He'd never told them to wear khaki pants with tight black or white t-shirts, yet they all did.

"I want one man to stay with me for the rest of the day," Cuba said, pointing at a man wearing a white t-shirt. "The rest of you need to take up positions in and around the dock area. In the cafes, in the dive shops and tourist traps. We need to find Grace."

He knew they also needed to find Ernie and also the treasure, but one thing at a time for Cuba.

What's my intention with Grace? I need to figure that out, Cuba thought.

He wanted her by his side. He wanted to be the father she never had. Cuba wanted to make up for lost time, to explain he was in love with her mother and she was in love with him. Not with Ernie. That was a marriage of convenience and nothing more.

Cuba wanted to find the treasure and leave Mexico. With Grace. They'd live a wonderful life, traveling the world together and seeking new adventures.

He knew where the treasure was, but he was worried he'd been wrong. The boats weren't near where he'd set the GPS coordinates on the yacht. That was miles away. Had he missed something, or was the map they had been a fake?

Cuba thought maybe the map he'd seen was the fake.

The cartel boats were using a grid pattern to find the crew of the sunken boat now.

"We'll need eyes on the cartel boats, too," Cuba said to his men. A couple of them nodded in unison.

If he had time he'd look for more men to hire for this task, since this might end in violence and bloodshed. More than likely since the cartel was involved.

As long as Grace is safe, Cuba thought.

In the next two days he'd see if there was a gap in all of these moving parts and perhaps do a solo dive on the wreck. Hope he hadn't buried it when he'd had the yacht sunk. Maybe it was right there and all of this running around and playing this chess game would mean nothing.

Let them all fight over nothing, Cuba thought.

While they were circling one another, he'd haul a treasure chest or two onto his own boat and sail away with it. No one would even know.

Cuba smiled as they started to turn back toward the marina. Soon they'd all be in place and watching for the cartel to give up the hunt and arrive as well.

He really hoped they didn't have Grace with them. He was interested to see what they'd do with Ernie Patek, since one of his men had spotted the fat man onboard one of the cartel boats.

"I'll need some food, too," Cuba said. "We'll eat quickly and then get back to work. This is going to be an interesting rest of today."

Cuba gave a quick wave as the cartel boats got smaller and smaller.

THIRTY-NINE

There was a man in Ohio who had forged a Rembrandt. Ernie didn't know which one. He wasn't an art connoisseur and only cared about it if he could make money selling pieces. But he knew Rembrandts were worth millions. Rembrandt's paintings were also the most stolen out of any artist's works hanging in galleries.

The man in Ohio had painted, aged, and framed the Rembrandt all on his own. Then he had broken into a gallery, bypassing all security measures, and swapped the real one for the forgery.

The fake was so good that, fifteen years later, nobody was aware that they were staring at a fake.

This man was Ernie Patek's younger brother, which was the only reason Ernie knew about this. In underground crime, his brother was the go-to-man for anything that needed to be forged. The Secret Service had been chasing him for decades, but they didn't even know who they were chasing. His brother was a shadow.

So when Ernie came to him and said he needed an authentic looking treasure map, something about a century old, his brother went right to work. For a price, of course. Just because he was family, didn't mean he was owed any favors.

Ernie didn't mind paying, though. It would be well worth it. He knew once he gathered his men and made it down to that little beach town in Mexico, word would get out that he was there. He also knew that people talked, especially drunk people, and that at some point one of the men he brought with him may inadvertently mention they were treasure hunting.

And what did Americans in Mexico looking for treasure bring? The cartel.

The only thing Ernie needed to make sure of was that he was the only person who knew the map was fake. That way, when the cartel eventually showed up, he could pretend to partner with them and give them the map in good faith. Meanwhile, he'd have Cuba bring a couple guys to the actual wreck site.

Unfortunately, the tall piece of ass who'd been hanging onto him had grabbed the map before he could negotiate with the cartel.

Now, he found himself sitting on a boat in the ocean, hands tied behind his back, and a half dozen cartel members around him shooting into the water.

Ernie had recognized the boat in the distance as one of his. He'd been wondering when Cuba was going to come find and rescue him. It had taken him long enough. But then he watched as the boat turned around and drove off back toward the shore.

Ernie knew he wasn't the smartest person in the world, or even on the boat, but he realized the real reason Cuba had shown up. Despite Ernie handing Cuba coordinates to program into the yacht, not thinking that Cuba would want to know where it led, he must have still believed the map was real. Cuba wanted the treasure like everybody else.

Ernie groaned and ducked his head, letting the blazing sun burn a different part of his exposed skin.

With Cuba going behind his back, Ernie had nobody to try to take him from the cartel. Even though Maria, her ass two feet from his face, was gorgeous, she was also ruthless. Ernie thought Raul was the one he needed to watch for, but Maria was even more dangerous.

All of this only meant one thing to Ernie: he was going to die.

At some point, whether he led them to the actual treasure location or not, they would kill him. And he had a feeling that after they were done killing him, Maria and Raul were going to leap at each other like tigers in a cage.

Ernie wanted to feel bad that Grace would be left without her father, but that wasn't technically true. Besides, she never really seemed to care for him anyway. Maybe something biological had been keeping her from ever really treating him as a daughter should.

"Nothing so far," Raul said.

Ernie watched the other cartel boats slowly going up and down the water, searching for whoever had been on that flaming pile of mess sinking in the water.

"The other boat is leaving. Should I send one of ours to follow?" Raul asked Maria.

"No. Whoever that is can be our problem later. Right now we need to find those people."

Ernie looked at the DEA agent next to him. He seemed to have given up already. It was the same as any of Ernie's experiences with government men. They lost all motivation once something went wrong.

"Why do you need them?" Ernie asked.

Maria turned around and looked him up and down. "Were you staring at my ass?"

"Maybe. But why do you need to find these people?"

"Not that I owe you an answer, but they obviously have the map. Since you seem to be next to useless, I'd prefer to have the map than your shoddy memory."

"Just go to the wreckage. They seemed to be anchored there for a while. Wouldn't it make sense that they were anchored about where the map told them to go?" Ernie looked at his surroundings. "In fact, those two peaks in the distance look familiar. And over there, that reef. I think I remember now. We must be near it."

Maria looked at Raul, who shrugged and told his man to navigate to what was once Alberto's boat.

Ernie leaned back against the side of the boat and allowed himself a smile. Money can make stupid people do stupid things, but it could make smart people do even worse. He just hoped the two men he'd sent out to this site on the map when they had first landed in the country had done their jobs well.

When the boat reached the area, they anchored.

"There's definitely something down there," Raul said, looking at the underwater sonar.

Once Maria and Raul visibly confirmed that there was some kind of wreck under them, they kicked things into full gear, getting a couple men suited up and in the water. All thoughts of finding the people who'd abandoned their ship were put behind them.

Ernie knew gold rush fever when he saw it.

The two men went into the water. Raul, for the first time that Ernie had seen, smiled, and for a brief moment any tension between Maria and Raul seemed to dissipate.

"You know, since I brought you guys to the treasure, it's time we should talk about my cut," Ernie said.

"Oh don't worry. You'll be getting everything you deserve." Maria turned away from him and spoke into the radio.

One of the two divers confirmed they had just reached the wreck. Definitely a wooden ship, nothing modern looking. They were making their way throughout the broken mess.

"Hold on. I see something. It's a box. Some sort of wooden box. Metal clamps. No lock that I can see," the voice from the walkie said.

"Don't open it, idiot. Bring it up to the surface," Maria said.

"I figured if I'm going to die, I might as well take a couple of you with me," Ernie said.

Maria and Raul turned to him, but with a confused look on their face. Maria was about to speak when the water all around them lit up and a loud, but muffled sound came from underneath them.

A giant spout of water shoved the boat sideways and showered everyone. Everyone on the boat was knocked to the floor. Ernie took a hard hit, but didn't notice.

The pressure release bomb he had had his men set up under the fake treasure chest had worked. Obviously.

Maria and Raul were screaming at each other, at the remaining men on board, and at Ernie. But Ernie wasn't paying attention.

He was too busy laughing.

FORTY

Cuba hadn't even finished his coffee when one of his men called to tell him the survivors of the torched boat had been spotted a few miles north of town.

Likely someone saw them and wanted to make a few dollars, so they gave them up, Cuba thought. Everyone was on the take and everyone had a price.

"I'll take this coffee to go and give me half a dozen more. Quickly," Cuba said. He'd told his men to follow them at a safe distance. He wanted to be the one to intercept them, but he was also worried the cartel was close behind, too. No sense in having a shootout in public if they could help it.

He also notified all of his men to meet him there, because if there was trouble he needed to make sure he had enough weapons and shooters to even the odds.

The cartel has unlimited resources, and the Mexican police in their pocket. I'll need tens of thousands of loyal men to even the odds, Cuba thought.

As he drove to the GPS coordinates he smiled. This was going to be some gathering. He'd need to sort through who was with Grace and if they were important or not.

If any of them had a use he'd let them live. Otherwise he didn't need more hostages and people getting in his way. He doubted any of them knew Grace for longer than a few days, so likely not some fellow Americans.

Cuba arrived and waited in his SUV on the side of the road as the figures moved from the small beach toward the pavement.

He knew his men were all around the area, so no matter what Grace and her new friends weren't going to go too far.

As they got closer and saw the SUV, the group stopped.

Cuba stepped out, making sure they all saw the Glock in his hand. "Grace, honey, come on over. Bring your friends. I'd like to meet them."

Three of his men stepped out from their hiding places so everyone was on the same page.

"Cuba? Uh, hey," Grace said, glancing at her companions.

One of them, a small child, might be dead. He was being carried.

They looked waterlogged and tired. None of the group put up a fight, simply climbing into the SUV. Grace got up front.

"We need to go to the hospital for Ignacio," Grace said to Cuba. She put a hand on his arm. "Please."

"Is he still alive?" Cuba asked, glancing back at the three people in the backseat.

"We don't really know, since none of us are doctors," the pretty woman said.

Cuba waved one of his men over. "Take the child to the doctor. See if he can be fixed. Hurry."

"Thank you," Grace said. She introduced her companions, two of them Americans. The boat captain, Alberto, was known to Cuba by reputation. The best captain in the area by far. It made sense he'd be involved in all of this.

Cuba wasn't worried any of them would try something stupid. They knew they were wanted by the cartel and were lucky he'd found them.

Out of the frying pan and into the fire, Cuba thought. He began driving as soon as the boy was taken by his men. He knew the child was already dead but it would mean a lot to Grace if he tried to help, a small thing to him.

"Let's not confuse what's happening right now, okay? You are my guests but you are also my prisoners," Cuba said and smiled. "Until we figure out what is happening. I'll need to chat with all of you, individually, and see what you know or don't know."

"Thanks for picking us up, I guess," Rick said. "As prisoners, will there be good food and showers, dry clothes and some cold beer, or are we getting a deep, dark dungeon with bread and water?"

Cuba shook his head. "We're too low on the water table for there to be proper basements. If we were up north somewhere I'd say there would be a solid chance of it." He chuckled. Might as well be nice to these people, who knew they were controlled by him right now. "I had a finished basement when I lived in New York as a teen. It was magnificent."

"New York? I thought I recognized the accent," JoJo said.

Another chuckle from Cuba. "Puerto Rico born and bred, but when I was twelve my parents split and I went to live with my papa in Queens. I learned a few important lessons in my formative years."

"Such as?" Rick asked.

"I learned the Mets were awful and I rooted for the Yankees. The streets are dangerous but if you get in with the right gang and pledge loyalty to their stupid causes, you have protection. I also learned mini-bagel sandwiches in Brooklyn at three in the morning cannot be beat. Those I mostly miss." Cuba kept his eye out for anyone except his own men following him or roadblocks ahead. He felt good he was the one who'd found them and not the cartel.

"My father will be so disappointed when he realizes you're on the wrong side," Grace said.

Cuba shrugged. "I think Ernie will understand, in the end, why I make the choices I make. Hell, if he were in my position he'd do the same. I'd be so disappointed if he didn't, in fact. We're all in this for the same thing." He glanced in the rearview mirror at JoJo. She was a bit older than he preferred but she still had sex appeal. "What about you, pretty woman? Why are you in this?"

"I think the same as you. We're all looking for the big score, and we all think we found it, only..." JoJo sighed. "Only I'm beginning to think we've all been duped."

"By who?" Cuba asked.

"Be Grace's father. I stole the map but wonder whether it's even real. I now wonder if any of this is real. We could be chasing a legend, a myth about a sunken ship and a lot of gold and silver, maybe," JoJo said.

"Or this could all be real," Cuba said. "I am a generally positive person, so I'll think I'm about to be very, very rich."

"By very, very rich you mean so much wealth you can share with a backseat of partners?" Rick asked.

Cuba shook his head. "I already have a crew. They are loyal to me and me only. They'll get paid handsomely for the work they do."

"Are any of them divers?" JoJo asked.

"Yes," Cuba said quickly. He knew a couple of them could make a dive but he didn't know their skill level. He knew his own, and knew he was more than capable of figuring it all out. "Why, are you offering your diving service to my cause?"

"And why can't it be our cause?" JoJo asked and grinned, catching Cuba's eye in the rearview mirror. "There should be more than enough to go around... if it even exists, of course."

"As I said... I think it does." Cuba was happy they'd arrived back at his villa without having any troubles. They didn't seem like they were followed, which was just as well.

They exited the vehicle and all went quickly inside. Cuba asked them to not sit on the furniture because he didn't want to pay for the cleaning bill.

"But you're about to be a multimillionaire how many times over?" Rick asked.

Cuba ignored the sarcasm and turned to Alberto. "Captain, you've been very quiet during all of this. Why?"

"I am trying to learn."

"Learn what?"

Alberto shrugged. "When you are planning to kill me."

FORTY-ONE

Baker didn't know what the hell was going on. He'd been spending his time in captivity on the boat thinking about the mess he'd gotten himself into, and hoping his wife would be taken care of when he was gone.

He had no doubt about his impending death. The cartel didn't just untie you, slap you on the back of the hand, and let you take the next United flight home.

One moment Baker was thinking back to the amazing vacation they'd taken to St. Kitts for their tenth anniversary, the next moment he was tossed from his seat and smashed his face into the other side of the boat.

That seemed to be his life lately: sometimes he'll feel like things couldn't be any better, and other times he'll break his nose against a fucking cartel boat.

How had he even made it into the agency? Granted, he was never picked to do this James Bond shit as a lone agent, but they must have seen something in him as an asset in order to hire him on. All he'd done since he'd been down here was make a botched attempt to hire a boat captain to help him get the treasure, been caught by the cartel, and get stuck on their boat, tied up next to Ernie fucking Patek.

The DEA had been after him for a long time, but could never find anything that would stick. Despite the man's size, he was like Teflon.

Now here was Baker, hearing Patek talk like he wasn't there from the moment he was brought into the cartel house until now, and there was nothing Baker could do. He wasn't here officially. If Baker was legitimately on vacation, instead of going behind the agency's back to try to improve his home situation, he'd be able to report it. More agents would be sent in, and he'd probably get some award and promotion.

But since he'd gotten himself into this stupid situation without approval, he couldn't say shit. At the least he'd be canned. At worst, possibly jailed. Baker wasn't sure if what he was doing was that much of a criminal offense.

Baker got on his knees and watched as blood poured out of his nose onto the floor. He looked around, breathing through his mouth and occasionally spitting out blood when he lifted his head too high.

The guy driving the boat was out cold, the windshield next to where he sat cracked and smeared with blood. Raul and Maria were both on the ground, dazed but attempting to shake it off. Ernie had landed against the tied up life vests and appeared to be perfectly fine besides his maniacal cackling.

Baker heard splashing and yelling. He looked over the side of the boat and saw two men in the water. Both apparently had no idea how to swim and each were fighting to use the other as a floatation device.

Fuck them, Baker thought.

"Patek. Patek." Baker tried to get Ernie's attention without yelling.

Finally, Ernie stopped laughing and looked in Baker's direction. Baker gestured toward Raul, who was closest to Ernie.

Patek was no fool, though he was known for being a bit dull in the head. Baker watched as Ernie picked up his bulk, took two steps toward Raul and basically did a modified elbow drop on the guy. Raul stopped moving.

Baker turned to Maria, who was gaining her wits back faster than he expected. She saw what happened with Raul and turned to Baker.

He dropped on his back, lifted both knees to his chest, and shot out his feet, kicking her in the face and knocking her out.

"I'm sorry. I don't hit women," he said, though she couldn't hear him.

Baker looked at Ernie. He had taken a pocket knife from Raul and was working blind at cutting his hands free. When he finished he went over to Baker and cut his ties off as well.

"I wouldn't usually help out a NARC, but we'll have to team up to get out of this situation. We help each other and then both go our separate ways. Agreed?"

"Agreed."

Ernie patted Raul down, taking his gun, another knife, and a smaller gun in an ankle holster. He walked over to Maria, but Baker stopped him.

"I'll do it. You'll just be all creepy and grope an unconscious woman."

"And that thought didn't cross your mind?"

"No I ... no it didn't."

After checking Maria, they tied both of them up and dragged them down to one of the bedrooms. After searching the boat and finding more rope, they lashed Maria to one of the beds, and Raul to the toilet. Ernie got a kick out of that.

Baker followed Ernie upstairs onto the deck and before Baker had time to process what was going on, Ernie shot the two men still floundering in the water, then shot the driver point blank in the head and tossed him over.

Ernie, breathing heavy, looked at Baker.

"Fuck 'em," Ernie said.

"Yeah. Fuck 'em." Baker never thought he was one to be so casual about murder, but these people were scum.

He was a little worried that Ernie had a gun and he didn't. He was also surprised that he found no weapons on Maria. Baker would think the head of this arm of the cartel would be constantly armed.

Maybe she was confident in her position and the loyalty of her men. Maybe she was underestimating the pull of power that would cause someone like Raul to blow her head off and take over.

Whatever the reason was, it left him unarmed. Baker was not comfortable with that. He made sure to stay close, but behind Ernie as he started turning the boat around and heading to shore. At least that way, if Ernie decided to attempt to kill him before they got close to land, he'd have a fighting chance at stopping him.

Baker was definitely in better shape than Ernie, but you didn't have to be remotely athletic to pull a trigger.

"So, what are you going to do with the two downstairs?" Baker asked.

"I figured I'd leave that to you. You can call in your men or whatever it is you do."

Baker came close to telling Ernie he was on his own, rogue, and not even that great of an agent, but he kept his mouth shut.

"And you?" Baker asked.

"There's only one reason Cuba would show up where he did. He's looking to cut me out. And if he's looking to cut me out and make it out of the country alive, there's only one way he'd be able to do that."

"How's that?"

"He'd get a hold of the only thing that matters more to me than the fucking treasure. He's got my daughter. He's got Grace."

FORTY-TWO

"Time to lay the cards on the table," Grace said to Cuba, trying to sound and feel confident. She thought she knew the man but she'd underestimated his greed and drive.

Cuba shrugged and popped another shrimp in his mouth. "Sure. You should eat, too. We might have a couple of long days ahead of us. How'd you sleep?"

"I slept awful. These beds aren't made for people like me. The fact I'm a prisoner didn't help me, either." Grace ignored the food and drink on the table.

The pair were seated on one of the many decks overlooking the coast, just enough blue tinge to the horizon to let you know the Pacific was within driving distance.

It was beautiful. Grace wondered if her father or Cuba had actually rented it.

My father is Cuba, Grace thought. She needed to have a conversation with him. Maybe let him see her as his daughter and not a prisoner.

"What cards are you referring to? The fact I need to use you, as distasteful as that is, as a pawn in this chess game? The fact I betrayed Ernie Patek and want the treasure for myself? The fact I might have to kill your companions in order to get what

I want?" Cuba leaned forward and smiled. "Or the fact you are my daughter?"

Grace smiled back. "Yes to all of those questions and a hundred more."

"You already knew I was your father," Cuba said and took another shrimp from the plate. "How long have you known?"

"A long time. Not only did I understand the relationship between my mom and you early on, I knew Ernie was my father only on the birth certificate," Grace said. "Has it ever been openly discussed? I'm sure he knows about the affair."

Cuba nodded. "I think he has a strong gut feeling about it. As far as I know he never asked or accused your mother of anything before she died. He suspected, I'm sure. Especially since you tan so easily, right? You definitely don't have his complexion or genes and it is obvious."

"I thought you and Ernie were best friends. Grew up together. Had each other's back. What happened? Were you always an asshole or was my mother too much of a temptation?" Grace asked.

"Likely both. I was in love with her before your father even knew her name. I stepped aside when Ernie made it clear he was going to have her, and since he had all the money and I was a nobody, I deferred to him. Reluctantly." Cuba sighed. "He said it was too easy for me with my good-looks and my personality. He needed to show off his money to get a good woman. I could have a pick of all of them but he only got to work on a handful at most, in his entire life."

Grace shook her head. "I find it hard to believe my father didn't think he was God's gift to women."

"Not when we were growing up. In his twenties he overpaid for so many hookers because he felt like he wasn't worthy of a woman loving him for him." Cuba ate another shrimp. "Things just happened between your mother and I. Things meant to happen. Soulmates, maybe."

"Did she ever love him?" Grace asked, not wanting to hear the real answer and already knowing it. She'd known it for a long time, in fact. The way her parents interacted with one another, the way they used her as the buffer.

"I think in her own way she did. They got along. As a power couple they were unstoppable. Your mother was the definite brains behind everything he ever did, and she wanted to pass it down to you, until..." Cuba closed his eyes and popped another shrimp in his mouth. "You should eat something. Your friends are dining right now. I feed my guests well."

"So I'm a guest now?" Grace needed to process everything they'd talked about. There was nothing she didn't already know, but it was different actually hearing it from Cuba. "Would you and my mother have eventually run off together?"

Cuba shook his head. "No. Never. She was very adamant she enjoyed the life she had. Unless we planned to kill Ernie, which we never would, things were going to be as they were until the end. Even you being born didn't change any of that."

"Now will you kill Ernie? For a treasure chest of gold coins?"

Cuba smiled. "Is that what you think is at the bottom of the ocean? That would be tempting. I have to be honest."

Grace knew Cuba would kill Ernie to get what he wanted. Maybe it was because he'd never fully gotten the love of his life. He'd called her mother his soulmate. Perhaps this was his long way of getting everything he wanted, including getting rid of Ernie Patek.

"Tomorrow morning, bright and early, you and I will go diving together. Like old times," Cuba said and smiled.

"A normal daddy-daughter excursion. I imagine we're going to try to find the treasure," Grace said. "And if we do? Is that when you kill me and leave me on the bottom, or wait until we get the valuables back to the boat so you can kill me and the others all at once?"

"No one has to die," Cuba said and shrugged. "Seriously, I know you love shrimp. Eat some before they get cold."

Grace was hungry and not eating wasn't going to hurt anyone but herself. She filled a plate with a few shrimp and squeezed a couple of lemon slices onto them.

Cuba seemed satisfied when she started to eat. "When was the last time you dove?"

"The other day when the anchor got stuck on the shipwreck. Before that? Maybe three years. It's like riding a bike, though, right? I can do the basics with my eyes closed," Grace said. "Why are the two of us going down?"

"Trust."

Grace chuckled. "Wow. You trust me more than anyone else right now? That says a lot about your predicament. I guess none of your men are trustworthy enough to dive with you. Afraid they'll try to kill you?"

Cuba looked uncomfortable. "I didn't say that."

"You didn't have to. I wonder how many of them are still loyal to my father, or simply playing both sides to see who gets the treasure. Maybe one or two think they can simply take it themselves when all is said and done." Grace smiled again. She could see how uncomfortable Cuba was, and that was a good thing. It meant he was likely going to keep people alive and see how it played out and who was on which side.

It might also mean he'd kill everyone until he was the last man standing, Grace thought. "The group I am with are loyal to me. I can make them loyal to you if you let me. They'll help with the extraction of chests and whatever else is down there. Think about it. They just want a fair cut, and there should be more than enough for everyone. No way you can do it all on your own, especially with the cartel sniffing around."

"I'm not worried about the cartel or your father, really," Cuba said. "I'm worried about running out of time before new factions come into play. Word of something this monumental happening off the coast of Mexico will travel quickly, and I'm amazed there aren't already different groups landing as we speak."

Grace was worried about the same thing. This was all complex, with so many moving parts. She felt like it was going to get more intricate before they figured out what was down there.

FORTY-THREE

Maria awoke to something rattling and banging. From the way her head felt, it could have been coming from inside her skull, but as she became more aware, the noise was clearly in the room with her.

In the room? Why was she in a room? And a small, smelly one, at that.

She went to wipe her blurry eyes and her wrists pulled back, banging against something solid. Maria looked above her head and saw her wrists tied to the pole of the bunk bed she was leaning against.

It came back to her in a second: the explosion; Ernie flopping on Raul like a beached whale; the U.S. agent kicking her in the face. They must have tied her up while she was out, which meant she was no longer in control.

Maria did not like not being in control.

The rattling and banging intensified, accompanied with some cracking noises and grunting.

"Raul?" No answer. "Raul, are you alive, or flopping around because the fat man shattered your bones?"

The noise stopped, replaced by heavy breathing.

"Give me a couple minutes to get out of this toilet, Maria. Then you can treat me like I'm beneath you all you want." The noise resumed.

"Tied to a toilet like the piece of shit you are," Maria mumbled.

"I heard that."

"Wasn't trying to hide it. Hurry up, my arms are going numb."

Raul's effort intensified, and in a few more pulls, Maria heard wood splintering and an exhausted gasp.

Raul walked into the room, a chunk of porcelain still clinging to his wrist ties. His hair and face were soaked and blue from the toilet water. Maria could have laughed if she wanted to, and she wanted to more than anything. But the look in Raul's eyes told her that he would pummel her to death if she did.

Hell, she was tied up to the bed. He might do it anyway, if he had the guts and the foresight to do it.

Raul grabbed the piece of toilet hanging from his wrists and sawed through the ties. He walked over to Maria and did the same.

Maria sat up and let her arms dangle by her side. The blood rushing back into her hands felt like fire.

"Are they up top? Ernie and the bastard who kicked me in the face?"

Raul shook his head. "I don't think so. I've been making enough noise the last ten minutes, someone would have come down. We haven't been moving either, so we're docked or anchored. If we're anchored they must have found a way off. Docked? They left us."

"Why would they leave us? They could have easily killed us and had nothing to worry about. At least for a while."

"Because they are not like us and that makes them weak. Weak and stupid. And easy to find and kill."

They went topside. The boat was empty, except for a patch of blood dried against the cracked and spiderwebbed glass by the driver's seat.

The boat was tied up at the dock. Not the one Maria was used to launching off of. This one was older, more... peasant. But there was nobody waiting for them. She guessed someone could be sitting at the old three-sided bar one-hundred feet down the beach, but what would be the point. Maria wasn't sure what Ernie was going to do, but if he was smart he'd get the hell out of the country fast. Which meant he was probably still around somewhere.

The other guy. The agent who looked like a fish out of water. He'd be long gone. Especially since Maria was pretty sure he wasn't here under any official capacity.

"Call the men in. Tell them to get here fast. We find Ernie first and kill the bastard. Then we go after the people that were on the boat. If they're still alive. Someone will know. And someone will know whose boat it was."

"What about the DEA agent?"

"He could be your side project. Not a real threat. Just a badge with no power behind it. Shouldn't be too taxing on you, Raul."

Raul scowled at her and headed to the bar to use their phone. If the owner was smart, he'd let him. If he wasn't, Maria would know by the gunshots.

Despite the set up with the fake treasure, Maria was certain Ernie Patek knew where the real loot was. It may not be saved in his head, but he knew where to find the information. He was the most important part.

The group was already out when they pulled up? Well, lucky for them they didn't dive the wreck before they abandoned ship. Unlucky for them, Maria didn't like loose ends.

Something buzzed on her hip and for a second Maria thought a bullet grazed her. Her nerves were so on edge, she expected anything to happen, even out in the open like she was. For all she knew, Raul had made a call and had someone nearby ready to take her out.

She knew they were both thinking of doing the same thing to each other, but the right time hadn't come, and when you pull big moves at the wrong time bad things happen.

Maria reached under her shirt and touched her sports bra. Between her breasts, the folded 4300 Composite Lite Auto blade held tight. They may have taken her gun, but it appeared nobody touched her tits. Which must have meant the agent searched her. Ernie's gross hands would have been all over her.

She pulled the knife out and held it in her hand as her hip buzzed again.

Her cell phone.

The morons took her weapon, but a phone could do more damage than a gun could.

Maria answered the phone. The voice on the other end spoke too fast, skipping words and barely making any sense.

"Pilar, calm down. I have no idea what you're saying. Take a deep breath. That's it. What's happening?" Before she answered, Maria already felt a pit in her stomach.

She listened to her sister go through the story, her blood pressure rising. Her ears felt clogged and her head felt like it was going to explode.

"How? How did this happen?"

Her sister told her as much as she was able to gather from the situation. Maria's hand tightened on the phone and she heard the plastic begin to crack.

"I'll be there as soon as I can. You make sure they know who they're dealing with and who's on the way."

Maria hung up without waiting for an answer.

Raul made his way back from the bar.

"They're on the way. Ten minutes. Where are we headed?" Raul saw her face as she turned to him. "What's going on, Maria?"

Maria pressed the button on her switchblade and glared into Raul's eyes.

"My son."

"Your son? You don't have a son. What are you talking about?"

"My sister raised him. I didn't need to have a kid around that some rival could use for leverage. But you or one of your idiot men shot him."

"What? We've been out on the water this entire time. How could we have shot some kid?"

"I have to go see him."

"Of course. The men will be here shortly. We'll get you to him."

Maria shook her head.

"No. You stay here." She swung her arm around and buried the blade into Raul's neck.

His eyes went wide and he bled out before he was fully on the ground.

Maria pulled the blade out and waited for her men to arrive. Whoever had shot Ignacio didn't matter. Raul was in charge, so it was his fault.

And now? Now he was in charge of nothing.

FORTY-FOUR

Cuba wasn't sure this was going to be the right move. There were so many locations that the treasure *could* be in at this point. There was no telling if any of them were the right one, or if the real X marks the spot was somewhere else.

He wished Ernie was here, if only to throttle the man until he told him where it really was.

"Stop looking at my daughter like that," Cuba said to Rick, watching the man openly stare at Grace's ass in her thong bikini.

Rick chuckled uneasily. He glanced at JoJo, who was also filling out a thong bikini nicely. "I have a hot chick already, buddy. Are we all cool with you and her being related now? It seemed like a big reveal that you all knew already. Seems weird, no?"

"Weird? Why?" Cuba motioned for Alberto to come over to him.

"For years you two knew the real relationship but kept it a secret, I guess from Ernie. Now that he's not around, it feels like at some point soon you and *your daughter* are going to run off and go to Disneyland or somewhere. Have a father-daughter date." Rick shrugged. "It's cute."

Cuba didn't like Rick. On multiple levels, he thought the man was an awful human being.

JoJo, on the other hand, had much promise. She was cunning. Sexy. Seemed in control no matter the situation. She would make a potential partner in the future if this all worked out the way Cuba thought it would.

Of course, if he was able to secure the treasure and it was even half of what he thought it would be worth, he might not need a partner. He could take his daughter to Disneyland and Disneyworld and all across the world, seeing all the sites. Living the good life.

No worries in the world at that point, Cuba thought.

All he needed to do was figure out where the treasure was underwater, and the only way to do it was to go underwater.

Alberto, eyes down, stood near Cuba.

"We need a new boat. Something fast and small," Cuba said. "Can you do this quickly and quietly? There will be spies everywhere, all looking for us. Looking for you, Alberto."

"Of course. I know someone. He owes me a huge favor," Alberto said.

"Then make it happen. I will secure tanks and equipment and we dive before dark tonight," Cuba said. He leaned close to Alberto. "I will cut you in for a fair share for helping, but if you even think about crossing me, I will slowly torture you to death. Your entire family will watch. Do you understand?"

Alberto nodded. He looked like he was going to cry.

Cuba smiled and patted Alberto on the shoulder. "Go. You have two hours. One of my men will accompany you, so there is no trouble."

And you do not start any trouble for me, Cuba thought.

Cuba gathered everyone around as soon as Alberto and one of his men left to secure a fast boat. "I have a plan and I'll need your help for this to truly work."

Rick smiled. "And then you'll kill us? I'm not sure I want to be helpful."

"I give you my word, if you both help me, I will give you a fair cut and you can walk away," Cuba said, looking at JoJo. "If that is what you really want."

JoJo gave Cuba a quick grin before looking away, and looking flustered.

She knows I want her, Cuba thought. "If you don't help me, I will have to kill you. Simple fact. We'll also never get the treasure to split, so everyone loses. And with my luck, Ernie Patek and the cartel will be splitting the treasure and laughing at our expense."

"I guess we really have no choice," JoJo said. "I hope you at least have a plan."

Cuba nodded. He knew if JoJo was in, Rick would go with the flow. Alberto had been threatened and Grace was his flesh and blood, so she would follow along.

Maybe I won't have to kill anyone. Maybe there will be enough for all of us, Cuba thought, but he doubted it. There was never enough and there was no honor among thieves.

"The original site I had on the yacht's GPS might not be a fake location. Maybe it was the actual one," Cuba said. "There's only one way to find out. We dive it."

"And if it's not? Do you really have other possible locations?" Rick asked. He seemed genuinely interested and not being sarcastic.

"I do. Several, in fact. I'll need a couple of days to look at the right maps, but I'm sure I can figure it out." Cuba smiled. "We know it is down there. Where? We need to find out." He made sure to keep saying we instead of I, so they felt ownership of this. So they were comfortable with him leading them, and so he could get one over on them when the time came.

"I'll dive," Grace said.

Cuba shook his head. "No. I need you topside to coordinate with Rick and Alberto."

JoJo smiled. "You want me to dive with you?"

"Of course. I think you already mentioned you were certified. You and I will go down with one of my men, who will document it for us. I have camera equipment we can use. Three in the water and three on the boat, plus my men," Cuba said.

"And what do I do?" Rick asked.

Cuba shrugged. "I'm guessing you know how to fire a weapon. You and my men will watch for the cartel, for Ernie, for pirates, for space aliens... whatever tries to get to us."

"I don't trust you but I guess I have no choice," Rick said, and glanced at JoJo, who shrugged.

"Then we wait for Alberto to get the boat. In the meantime, we need to eat and prepare for the dive. We might have several dives in the next few days, so perhaps a power nap is also in order," Cuba said.

"I'd like to head into town for a good cup of coffee and some food," Rick said.

Cuba laughed. "Oh, I'm sure you would. That is not going to happen. We all stay together. Joined at the hip for the next few hours."

Rick didn't seem surprised. Why should he? Cuba knew the man was testing the limit, seeing how far he could stray. Perhaps the man was smarter than he looked. He might have his own plan he was putting into motion, but the more Cuba looked at Rick the more he sensed the truth.

The man was a drug addict and likely wanted to go into town and get another fix.

Cuba wondered how long before Rick came crashing down from his addiction and was totally useless. Then he'd need to be disposed of quickly, before he was a distraction.

He wondered how someone so beautiful as JoJo put up with being around Rick. They were obviously fond of one another and Cuba guessed it was more than a simple grifter pairing. They'd been through Hell and back together and there was a bond.

I hope I'll be able to break that bond, make JoJo see what a waste Rick is, and side with me when the time comes, Cuba thought.

For now, they would wait.

"I'm hungry," Grace said. "Then I need to work on my tan."

Cuba smiled. "Let's go find my little girl something to eat in the kitchen. Rick... JoJo... join us."

He led the group downstairs, wondering what they were going to snack on. Wondering if Alberto could secure a fast boat without complications.

Wondering if he'd be rich in a few hours.

FORTY-FIVE

JoJo sat by the pool, her bare legs dangling in the clear water. The smell of chlorine mixed with the double Americano Cuba had made for her after they ate.

There weren't many houses close by and the stars in the night sky were clear and infinite. Unlike down on Earth, where everything going on right now was murky and could be very short-lived.

JoJo still hadn't addressed the elephant in the room with Rick. Even if she did believe that he hadn't started using again, just the fact that he had a bag on him was proof enough that he was, at some point, going to. Addicts rarely bought their drug and never used it.

She hadn't liked how she felt when Cuba looked at her either. Not that it felt bad, but just the opposite. She found it hard looking him in the eyes without feeling a twinge inside her. She knew without a doubt that she loved Rick, so why was she feeling these sudden emotions over some stranger?

Sure, Cuba was Hollywood handsome and built out of bricks and steel, but that had never been JoJo's type. She liked the unique, awkward looking men. Some features that were different from the standards of beauty.

Maybe she was just angry at Rick. Angry and frightened. She'd been around him when he was in the depths of his addiction and never wanted to see that person again. He'd made a lot of mistakes and gotten a lot of people in trouble because of it. But most importantly, he wasn't himself when he was high. JoJo loved Rick because of who he was, and the heroin buried all of that.

Maybe she was afraid of losing him and looking toward someone else to hang on to.

JoJo swirled her legs in the water and sipped her coffee.

Everything Cuba had brought up earlier made sense and seemed legitimate, but could they really trust Ernie Patek's ex-right-hand-man when it came to their lives?

JoJo had no idea which way to go. They obviously had no choice when it came to helping Cuba. But once they were in the water, a lot of things could shift in one direction or the other. The question was, should she go with the current that pulled toward a shore that benefited her and Rick more, or with the one that Cuba was offering?

JoJo had rarely been stuck for an answer when it came to anything in life, let alone anything on the other side of the law. But all she could do right now is sit at the pool and come up with nothing.

A long time ago, they'd helped an old friend's son disappear along with a ton of money that would hold him over until he was on his deathbed. That's where she thought her and Rick would be at this point. Instead, they were still scamming and scraping by, occasionally pulling in a big enough haul to not have to work the con game for a while, but nothing big enough to keep them out of it forever.

That's what she wanted. She'd always wanted that: to be able to do nothing. To disappear and relax for however many years she had left. Of course, that meant not being able to talk to people who knew your real identity, but the big score meant being alone. JoJo was fine with that.

The sliding glass door opened and closed. She didn't need to turn to know it was Rick. She'd recognize his gait anywhere.

He sat next to her, rolling up his pant legs and dipping his feet into the water. They were silent for a while, only the buzzing of the bugs and the distant crashing of waves made any noise.

JoJo wasn't going to make the first move.

"I guess we should talk, now that we have a second by ourselves," Rick said.

"You want to talk, then talk."

"I made a mistake. I know. But I didn't go through with it. I swear."

"But you would have, right? If it wasn't for that damn kid getting shot, you would have eventually used again."

Rick sighed and looked up at the sky.

"I'd like to say no, but honestly I have no idea. It felt... comforting just to have it on me. Kind of like someone who stops smoking but keeps a pack of cigarettes in the house. That knowledge that it's there is enough to keep you off it."

"Don't give me that bullshit, Rick. We've been through too much for any of that to fly by me. Heroin isn't cigarettes. And I told you when we first came down here that I was out the second you started using again."

"But I haven't."

"But you were thinking about it. Thinking about it to the point where you went out and bought a bag. That's like getting caught in bed with a naked woman, but saying it's okay because you didn't have sex with her."

They sat in silence again. JoJo heard laughing coming from the house. Probably Cuba and his men drowning themselves in tequila and saying stupid shit.

"So what do we do now?" Rick asked.

"We go with the plan and play it by ear. If we can find a way out, we take it. Otherwise, we find out if Cuba's full of shit or not."

"I meant with us. I saw how you looked at Cuba. Have I been that awful that you're thinking of leaving?"

"For Cuba? If you really think that, you don't need drugs to be high. It's nothing. I was pissed at you. And you have to admit, the guy's a looker."

"He is a handsome man, as much as it pains me to say it. It's just... I don't like how you were looking at him."

"Do you mean the way you were looking at Grace, or any other woman on the street with her ass hanging out? Typical machismo bullshit. Guys can stare at any woman they want, but the woman they're with can't look at another man without it puncturing your fragile ego."

"Pretty much."

JoJo laughed and slapped Rick's thigh.

"You're an idiot. But you're my idiot. Got it? Keep yourself straight. Don't bring any of that shit into the house again, and we'll be fine. You got your strike. You don't get a second one."

Rick leaned over and gave JoJo a kiss as the door to the pool opened.

"Hey, lovebirds. Time to fly. Alberto's back and he's gotten us a boat." Cuba said before shutting the door.

"You trust him?" JoJo asked.

"No."

"Me neither. We look out for each other tonight, ok?" JoJo put a finger against his chest and then hers. "The only two things that are important in this. Got it?"

"Got it."

JoJo got up and followed Rick into the house, hoping Cuba knew what he was doing. Still, she felt like she was walking into a trap, and once she was there it would be difficult to escape.

FORTY-SIX

Ernie Patek was sweating in this unbearable heat. He wished he had a bottle of tequila to get drunk.

"Cuba and I used to spend hours on the yacht drinking three, four bottles of tequila and talking about all of our big plans," Ernie said to Baker. "I was such a fool."

Baker shrugged and wiped sweat from his face. "We all do stupid things. Trust the wrong people. We need to find somewhere safe to hide. Regroup. Figure out who we can trust."

"No one," Ernie said. He rose slowly to his feet, pushing against the wall in the alley to keep from falling onto his fat ass. "We are on our own, unless you want to call in the calvary."

Baker shook his head. "There is no cavalry. I am a lone wolf in this. I'm also a fool. I thought I could do this on my own, figure out where the treasure was hidden and save my wife."

"Your wife?" Ernie was already walking down the alley. He wished they'd killed the cartel members instead of leaving them tied up on the boat, but he really had no choice. He didn't trust Baker and knew when it all came down, the DEA agent could say he watched Ernie kill innocent people and he was threatened by the man.

There are no innocent people in any of this, and Ernie knew it.

Ernie wondered if Baker was telling him the truth about not having backup. "Tell me about your wife." He glanced over his shoulder and watched to see if Baker's demeanor changed, which it did. The man looked... scared? Sad?

"She's very sick. My insurance doesn't cover much of anything. I need a miracle in order to get her the help she needs, but I tried everything," Baker said. "And then... I stumbled upon you and what an agent thought you were doing in Mexico."

"What agent?"

Baker sighed. "A DEA agent who's been following you for months. Years, likely. There's an entire group assigned to you."

Ernie stopped and turned back to Baker with a smile. "Really? How many agents?"

"I don't know the exact number."

"More than three? Five? Ten?" Ernie asked.

Baker nodded. "Maybe six or seven."

Ernie turned back and kept walking, satisfied there were so many men interested in what he was doing. And yet, none of them were lurking about and following as he did whatever he wanted to do. "We need to get out of this town. Maybe over to Mexico City. I have contacts there we can use."

"What about the treasure?" Baker asked.

"Since we didn't kill the cartel people, they will eventually get free and come after us. Hard. I'd rather not be here when it happens. Maybe they'll think we went back to the United States. They might think we got scared and fearing for our lives gave up," Ernie said.

"Cuba and your daughter will still try for the sunken treasure." Baker was now walking next to Ernie as they got out of the alley and onto a main street.

"We can only hope they create a distraction for us to slip away and live to fight another day." Ernie chuckled. "I'm not sure if I have any loyal men left in this town. I have to assume they're all working for Cuba now. Bastards."

"Maybe we should've killed Maria and Raul," Baker said quietly. "That would've been a nice distraction for us. Throw the cartel into chaos, even for a few hours or days."

"Except I couldn't do it, because I have a DEA agent tied to me," Ernie said and frowned. "If I find out you're setting me up to fall, I will come after you and your wife."

Baker pushed Ernie, who nearly toppled into the street. "Don't threaten me or my family."

"Not a threat. A promise. Let's just get away and regroup, ok? Time to cut our losses in the short-term and look at the long-term in all of this." Ernie didn't like Baker manhandling him, and doing it so easily. He knew he was grossly overweight but he had power and most people would be afraid to touch him, let alone give him an embarrassing shove. He would not forget Baker had done it, either.

They managed to walk halfway across town, until Ernie was sure they weren't being followed. Not by anyone important, anyway.

The street urchins kept tabs on everyone, and Ernie knew they'd eventually get the word back to the cartel about their route.

Not that it mattered. Ernie wanted to be in Mexico City and in an air conditioned room with a couple of Mexican hookers and a bottle of tequila by nightfall.

"Are there any DEA friends you have that might be interested in helping us out?" Ernie asked. It was worth a shot. Maybe Baker wasn't the only agent that could be bought, that would be interested in taking the treasure and splitting it instead of helping Uncle Sam.

"I'm not sure," Baker said after a long pause.

Ernie stopped near a restaurant on a corner and pointed at three cars parked on the curb. "Anyone interested in a long ride and a nice tip?"

All three drivers, all leaning against their vehicles, raised their hands and gave a smile.

Ernie was hoping to eliminate at least one if they didn't speak English. No matter.

"Baker, pick one and we ride," Ernie said.

He had U.S. dollars in his wallet, even though they were still wet. They were still good and went a long way in Mexico. He pulled out a hundred dollar bill and waited for Baker to pick.

"I don't care. Him," Baker said and pointed at the nearest driver.

"Perfect." Ernie leaned in close to the guy. "We need to get to Mexico City. Not a direct route. Understand? This is completely off the books, so don't call it in or whatever you taxi guys need to do. If you get us there in one piece and we're not followed, I'll give you another two hundreds. Deal?"

The driver nodded with a grin and opened the back door of his vehicle.

"I need to call my wife but I lost my phone," Baker said.

"As soon as we get to Mexico City I'll buy you a burner phone so you can call your sick wife and anyone in the DEA who would be interested in helping us with our little problem," Ernie said. "You'll have a few hours to think about who you want to contact."

Baker nodded and slipped into the car, Ernie right behind him.

Ernie would need to deal with Cuba and Grace at some point, and he wasn't looking forward to it. He knew how focused Cuba could be when he wanted something.

He took my daughter back. He took my wife many times in my own bed. Now he will take the treasure from me, Ernie thought.

"Smile, Baker. This is a fun adventure we're on. How many people can say they had such an exciting week, even in law enforcement? We've been shot at, right? Threatened. Kidnapped. Nearly drowned. A lot has happened, but we're still alive to tell our grandkids about it," Ernie said.

"I don't have children or grandchildren." Baker closed his eyes and leaned back. "I need some sleep."

Ernie slapped him lightly on the shoulder. "Get in a power nap. I'll wake you as soon as we arrive. Then we begin putting this all back together."

It would be a lot of work. Ernie would need to get more cash and quickly, so he could spread it around and get intel about what was happening in this town they were finally leaving.

Of course, if Cuba or the cartel got their hands on the treasure, he'd need to come up with another plan.

FORTY-SEVEN

Maria had no problem getting in to see Ignacio. The people at the hospital who didn't know her by face, knew her name.

The doctor answered all her questions, assuring her that he was injured but would be fine. He was stable and resting.

He was sleeping when she got to his room. Her sister was sitting by the bed, watching some soap opera on the television. Maria motioned for her not to say anything. She didn't want her son waking up and seeing her. Although she wanted to run up to the bed and hug him, the fact that he thought of her as his aunt pained her every time he called her that.

One day. One day he'll know the truth and it will either turn him against her or bring him closer. Maria was afraid it might be the first option.

She stared at Ignacio and watched him sleep for a few minutes before turning around and leaving the room. Since the doctors assured her everything would be okay, it was time to move on to bigger things.

Or, at least, time to make sure she wasn't going to be hunted. Sure, Raul was below her in rank, but he had many friends in higher places who might not take it lightly that she'd killed him. Especially over a matter that had nothing to do with cartel business.

Maria felt a hand on her shoulder and she reacted without thinking, almost punching her sister in the face and breaking her wrist.

But Pilar knew better than to surprise Maria. They'd grown up together until their parents split and Maria went with her father, while Pilar stayed in a small bungalow with their mother and the pittance her father sent them every few weeks.

Pilar pulled away and dodged the punch.

"Jesus. Why are you coming up behind me like that?"

"You're in a hospital. Are there safer places?"

"Safer than a place where people die more often than they do on the streets? You know my life, Pilar. Safety is temporary, and definitely not out in the open."

"He asks about you, you know. I don't know if he knows, or just has a suspicion, but he asks after his Aunt more than most kids should."

"He doesn't know anything. Unless you tipped him off, there's no way he could. And you know how important it is that it remains that way until he gets a bit older."

"You mean how old you were when Papa took you and abandoned me and Mama?"

"You had a choice. Don't try to blame me for your decisions."

"Yeah, a choice to leave Mama alone or not. That's not a choice and you know it, Maria. You were always his favorite anyway. You were born with something broken in you. Just like Papa. Just like your son. You want to know how he might know the truth? He sees the same thing in you. Running around like a street urchin, coming home thinking I don't know how he gets his money."

"Whose fault is that? You raised him. You let him run around and do whatever he wants. You're the bad mother for not putting your foot down, not me. I left to keep him out of this life. You let him go out on those streets and find it himself."

Maria noticed the group of nurses at one of the stations looking their way. She grabbed her sister by the arm and led her around the corner into a small, empty waiting room with the same crappy soap opera playing on the television mounted in the corner.

"Sit. Coffee?" Maria asked, gesturing at the dated and faded coffee machine.

Pilar shook her head and Maria shrugged. She dropped her coins in and pressed a couple buttons. The cup fell and wobbled, but stayed in place as the coffee poured into it.

Maria took a sip and turned to her sister.

"I've asked a lot of you. I know that. And this? This situation we're in now? It's more than you should have to go through." Maria took another sip of coffee before tossing it into the garbage. "I just need you here, just a little while longer. Things are a bit crazy right now, and I think I need to get away for a little while until it cools off a bit. But when I come back, it'll be for something big. Something that will change all of our lives."

"This is about that stupid treasure hunt, isn't it?"

Maria stared at her sister. "How do you know about that?"

"Ignacio. You forget, Maria. I raised him. We talk like family because we are more family than you and I. You may be his actual mother, but which one of us is really the mother here?"

"You're right. For now. I need to go away for a little while. Make some calls. Make sure things are alright. I did something out of emotion instead of using my head."

"How long will you be gone?"

"Hopefully not too long. Pilar, if things aren't alright, they will come for me. And no matter where I go, they'll find me eventually. And if this happens, Ignacio can never know about me."

"You think I would ever tell him? If it was up to me, he'd never know. But he'll find out. No matter if you live long enough to tell him, or you die and he finds out when he eventually gets involved with the wrong people–which will happen. Then he'll hate me and revere you as a martyr."

"Pilar ..."

"All you've done in your life is cause our family trouble. You want to run and hide, go run and hide. But I think it would be much better to stay and face whatever karma you have coming your way."

Maria would have slapped her sister if it wouldn't have just proved her point. Instead, she stood up straight and stared at her sister. A look that, no matter how older Pilar was, always withered her and reminded her who Maria was and what she was capable of.

"I'll call you when I can get a clean phone. I don't expect to be gone for long, but I do expect to be updated on my son's condition."

"What about this treasure situation? If it's real."

"It's real. And the others may go for it while I'm away. But I know who they are, so if they do get it, they won't have it for long. I should have waited to begin with. Let them do all the work and pull it out of the water. Then just take it."

"It's always been about money for you, hasn't it. Not family. Nothing but money."

"Money and power. Without power, your money is meaningless." Maria straightened her shirt and turned her back on her sister, just as she had done when her father had taken her away. "Answer your phone when I call. And remember your place in this family."

Maria walked out of the hospital and got into the rental car she'd procured under one of a couple aliases the cartel weren't aware of. Once any heat over Raul's death cooled off, she'd come back. And Ernie, the DEA, and those expat gringos weren't going to get in her way this time.

FORTY-EIGHT

Cuba could see Grace was furious she wasn't going to be part of the diving expedition today. As much as he thought she had the skills for it, he needed an ally on the boat while he was down there and vulnerable.

He hoped he could trust his own daughter.

JoJo was definitely being flirty with Cuba, and he was enjoying it. They helped one another with the scuba gear, hands casually rubbing against exposed flesh. At one point she'd bumped a knee lightly into his groin and smiled, apologizing.

Cuba noticed Rick looked annoyed, which made this all the more fun.

Rick, Grace and Alberto were remaining on the boat along with three of Cuba's men.

"If anyone gets out of line, take care of it," Cuba had said to his trio, knowing he'd already given them instructions before they'd been onboard the boat. Under no circumstances were they to harm Grace, even if she turned against them. They could subdue her but nothing more.

Cuba smiled as Rick cocked his head at him, as if daring the other man to say something sarcastic. Rick didn't scare Cuba but he knew a drug addict either high or looking for a high, was a danger. If he resurfaced in an hour and Rick was dead Cuba wouldn't lose any sleep.

Then he could make his move on JoJo, too.

"Ready when you are," JoJo said. She got into position on the side of the boat, ready to fall back into the water and begin.

Cuba gave a nod to his other diver going down with them. This man had been given private instructions to keep an eye on JoJo while they were exploring the shipwreck. No sense in being careless, especially if Cuba thought he was so close to finding the treasure.

Confident they were ready, Cuba went under and adjusted so he was comfortable. He followed the line down to the wreckage, hoping the yacht had fallen not directly onto the original ship. That would make this infinitely harder to search but he was confident it could still be done.

Cuba gave JoJo a quick thumb's up as the two wrecks came into sight.

Luckily, the yacht had missed the original wreck by less than ten feet. It might be covering some of the scatter zone but overall Cuba thought it was a good sign.

He motioned with his hand for JoJo to stay with him. They would search together. He didn't want her to find the treasure alone and then act like it wasn't here and try to come back later for it.

Cuba wondered what he'd do if it was actually down here, waiting for them to hook it and get it to the surface.

They cast their light onto the surface of the shipwreck. As a teen, Cuba would often dive on wrecks with friends. He was always amazed at what they'd find, even if it was nothing more than a shard of pottery or a bent metal spike. He thought in another life he was an archaeologist.

Right now he was a treasure hunter, and he only had money in his thoughts.

JoJo swam past and below him, giving Cuba a great view of her ass. He noticed his other man was also paying attention, too.

They combed the shipwreck, looking for large holes to get inside if possible. The boat had broken apart, either initially or over the decades, and was listed to its starboard side.

JoJo was pointing and Cuba saw it a second later: a very large hole in the side of the boat. Even after all this time in the Pacific Ocean, the wood hadn't completely disintegrated. There was a lot of metal scattered as well, and Cuba had a very bad feeling.

This isn't an actual ancient boat. It might be a fake, a fugazi, a ship created to look like it was really old, Cuba thought.

Not that it mattered, because he realized the truth of the matter... There was no record of a shipwreck here, in this spot, so it could be a thousand years old or a year old. The timeline didn't matter if there was treasure inside.

If this was more of a modern boat, it could still contain ancient treasure. Hell, it might have boxes of newly minted gold bars. Maybe even containers filled with diamonds from secret mines in Africa. It could be anything.

JoJo waited for Cuba near the entrance.

He nodded and went inside, slowly, hoping his other man would keep watch on JoJo and not just her tight ass. If she was going to try something, this might be the perfect spot to do it.

Cuba took his sweet time, knowing he still had at least fifteen minutes of air left. He moved inch by inch, trying not to disturb anything. The interior was filled with silt and sand, and there were many sea creatures making their home inside.

He caught a glimpse of something big across the boat, exiting through another large hole. It was likely a shark, but it was too big to be an Atlantic sharpnose shark, common in these waters but only growing to about four feet long. Cuba didn't want to dwell on what lair they were entering, and if the resident was going to try to get them to leave.

Cuba shone the light back and forth, but there was nothing inside the boat that looked like a treasure chest or any type of box.

JoJo was moving to their left, also searching.

We're not done yet. Maybe the treasure was tossed from the ship, Cuba thought.

He went to the other side and to the other hole and began a new search, waving his hand to move the silt out of the way.

Cuba pulled out the small metal detector he had clipped to his belt, cursing he hadn't used it earlier or inside the boat. As soon as he turned it on, though, it began to beep and buzz.

There was a lot of metal on the sand and in the rotting wood of the ship, and on closer inspection none of it looked ancient.

Modern nails. Dammit, Cuba thought.

This might even be a ship that was sunk on purpose, so the fish and sea life could begin to create a new reef, Cuba thought. He'd never done too much research, only looking for shipwrecks in the area.

Cuba kept using the metal detector, but it was useless with all of the debris.

JoJo swam nearby, also searching. The other man was waving his hands, but now there was so much sand in the water it was hard to see.

Cuba checked his time and sighed. He tapped JoJo on her leg and motioned for them to head up. JoJo nodded and they began their ascent.

They slowly followed the guide rope back up, making their stops when necessary.

Cuba wondered if they should even attempt a second dive in the area. His gut told him this was a dead end, but then... where could they hit next?

He'd have Alberto get them side-scanning radar and they'd begin doing a tight pattern in the area to see if there was another wreck.

This could take several days or weeks, Cuba thought. *It will be winter soon and the storms will pick up, making a search impossible.*

He felt like having to wait the winter out might put them behind the eight-ball. The cartel wouldn't worry about choppy waves, storms or putting their divers in jeopardy. They would only focus on the treasure.

No, Cuba needed to quickly regroup and figure out what the next move was going to be.

FORTY-NINE

Baker could barely breathe. It was hot in Mexico City. The kind of heat that made the seaside town they came from seem like a walk-in freezer. The heat and the altitude was making him very uncomfortable.

Ernie, who surprisingly seemed unaffected by the conditions, brought him to an oxygen bar, where they currently sat breathing in humidified oxygen and enjoying a strong Mezcal drink. Baker was still having problems catching his breath, but it was slowly getting better.

"I thought the plan was for us to go our separate ways," Baker said between deep breaths.

Ernie turned to him, not strapped to a tank, but definitely tanked.

"I think we can both help each other. Your connections and my money would go a long way. It would definitely benefit your wife." Ernie tapped the side of his glass and gestured to the man working there to refill his drink. "Never hurts for me to have an inside man, either."

"Why would you think I'd work with you? I took an oath to protect our country."

"First off, we're not in our country. Second, you took a pretty long ride with me to here and we're sitting in some hipster oxygen bar drinking Mezcal. Did you see the line of Tesla's outside? Third. . . I think you can answer that question yourself. What's more important: your country or your family?"

Baker took the cannula out from his nose. He didn't know if it was the pure oxygen, the booze, or the altitude that was making him light-headed, but the fog in his head was lifted. He felt a sudden rush of euphoria. Patek was right. What had his country ever done for him besides provide shitty healthcare and a paycheck that was taxed to hell?

The oxygen cut off and Baker looked at Ernie. Ernie made another motion to give him a second round.

"What about the treasure? You're going to leave everyone there to get it?" Baker asked.

Ernie laughed. "I doubt they'll be able to get it. They don't even know what they're looking for. Everyone is so focused on gold or silver that they're going to overlook the obvious staring them in the face. The treasure is safe for now."

"So I'm still not clear what we're doing here."

"Think for a minute. How am I going to get the prize across the border without it being confiscated? You have free reign to go in and out. No searches. No questions."

"So you're using me. What's to say you don't screw me over at the end?"

"Same logic, Baker. If I screw you over you have enough on me to put me in cuffs. We stick together and we both make out well."

They sat in silence for a while. Baker put his oxygen back on, moving the tube to sip at the delicious drink. The front of the oxygen bar was open, no windows, nothing closing it. It looked out into the street and they both watched the cars drive by. People walked past them going on their way to a job or a meeting, or something.

Baker thought about calling his wife. It had been a while and she was probably worried about him, even though she had bigger things to think about. He'd been on leave from the DEA for too long, though. Would they start tapping his phones? Would calling his wife lead them straight to Mexico City?

Baker had read all the files they had on Ernie Patek. Even before he made his way down, he was obsessed with the case that they had been building against him.

He knew all about the guy, including the guess on the DEA's part that his daughter wasn't actually his daughter. Baker didn't know if Ernie was aware of this or not, and it wasn't something he wanted to bring up at the moment. If it would benefit him in the future, he'd use it as a bargaining device, but for now it was best not to lay out all his cards.

"How are you going to get the loot out from the cartel if they find it first?" Baker asked.

"I'm not worried about that. Cuba will get to it first, if anything. If the cartel somehow beats him to it, I have my ways of dealing with that. Why do you think they took me but didn't kill me?"

"You have something on them. On at least one of them. Maria, I'm assuming. That's the only way you could be so calm right now. Whatever info you have is enough for them to not take you out."

"Close enough. And don't ask. We may be able to work together, but I'm not giving you everything I have."

Baker took a couple deep breaths from the oxygen and stood up.

"I think I'm good now. Let's go do whatever it is you have planned to do here."

"Don't you want to finish your drink?"

"I'm good. Would rather have a bourbon. This mezcal tastes a little too much like scotch. Not my favorite."

"It's booze. How is it not your favorite?" Ernie stood up and grabbed Baker's drink and downed it.

Ernie paid the bill and walked out to the bustle of the Mexico City streets. There seemed to be no order to the traffic. Too many horns and too many cars swerving about. Ernie had let the driver go when they'd gotten to the oxygen bar. He mentioned where they were going was close enough that they could walk.

Baker, though feeling better, was still getting out of breath as they made their way down the street.

"The hotel is right down the block. Don't worry, I got each of us our own rooms. Adjoining, so don't lock that door. I may have brought you in on this, but it doesn't mean I trust you yet."

They turned a corner and Ernie put a hand on Baker's chest and backed him up.

"What are you doing?" Baker asked.

"Shhh," Ernie said.

Baker took a look around Ernie and watched as a car door opened and someone stepped out.

"What the fuck is she doing here?" Baker asked.

They watched as Maria walked from the car into the same hotel they had booked a room in. Luckily, she didn't turn her head and see them.

"I knew we should have scuttled the boat and left them for dead. Goddamnit," Ernie said.

They waited as Maria walked into the hotel and disappeared.

"Well, shit. I guess we have to find a new place to go."

"What is she doing here?" Baker asked.

"You can never guess the cartel. She probably fucked something up and is now trying to run away with it."

"What does that mean for us?"

"Nothing. If anything it means we know where they are at."

Baker watched the head of the cartel walk into their hotel. The only thing he knew was that he was now involved with Ernie Patek, known in his field, and the Mexican cartel.

There were only a couple ways to get out of this situation and none of them looked good.

He turned with Ernie as they went to find another way to lay down low.

FIFTY

Catalina was waiting where Ignacio had told her to meet him, which was a good sign.

"You look unwell," the pretty girl said to Ignacio. "Shouldn't you still be in the hospital?"

He waved his hand dismissively, trying to seem tougher than he really was. He was glad they were on the beach and it was getting dark, because he was sure he looked even worse than he felt.

"Has anyone defected yet?" Ignacio asked. He knew the street kids had loyalty only to a certain line; after they'd been inactive for too long they'd either get the stupid idea to run their own gang or offer their services to a competitor.

"A couple. I'm sorry," Catalina said with a frown. "Leo and Arturo have joined with the dockside boys."

Ignacio groaned. "Then they will know what we've been after all this time. Leo and Arturo will have already told them about the treasure, and they'll come after me. Hard. They think I know where it is."

"And do you?" Catalina asked.

There was something in her demeanor that had Ignacio on high alert. She was trying too hard to be casual, too much trying to keep him at ease. This wasn't like her. Ignacio liked Catalina because she was no-nonsense. While he harbored romantic feelings for the girl, he knew it would never come to anything real. She was nearly a foot taller than him, and she liked a couple of the older boys. He'd confided in her about things in the past and she never asked questions, only listened.

Now she was asking the important question.

"I don't know where it is. I'm trying to find the treasure," Ignacio said.

Catalina tilted her head and he could see she looked sad.

He figured this was all falling apart around him now. His crew was going to splinter until there was nothing left, and they'd all watch to see if he knew where the treasure was.

Ignacio knew it was only a matter of time before they came for him. In his weakened state it would be easy to see if he knew or if he didn't.

Maybe I can enlist Aunt Maria to protect me, he thought. *She would know what to do.*

Ignacio decided against it for now, but he'd need to keep it in mind. The street urchins knew he was related to her but they'd still take the chance and come for him.

If they'd attempt anything, knowing he could have the cartel covering his back, Ignacio knew he was in trouble. He also knew there was a good chance they'd risk it, because there was treasure beyond your wildest imagination in the future. At this point, Ignacio wasn't sure which group was going to make the first move.

He knew his own crew was also likely to have already organized to force his hand and extract the information from him.

To be honest, once he'd been taken out of commission, even for a couple of days, he'd expected at least one of his top lieutenants to visit him in hospital with a subtle threat. Maybe even an out and out threat, explaining he'd never leave his hospital bed without divulging the location of the treasure.

Ignacio had played dumb for the past week but he knew where it was.

He kept his eyes on Catalina, forcing his thoughts away from the location of the single treasure chest he knew existed.

Right off shore, right near the desolate beach they were standing on.

At low tide the top of the chest could be seen. Only for maybe half of an hour, before the ocean swallowed and hid it again.

He didn't know how it had gotten here, if there was an actual shipwreck under the sand, if there were more than one chest.

So many questions for Ignacio.

The actual treasure map was useless, but the longitude and latitude written in light pencil on the backside of the map had led him here, only a few days ago.

He'd tried to open the chest but the lid was stuck, barnacles and sea life encrusted onto it. He'd need tools and a lot more muscle than he had to move it, even if he were able to dig it out.

Ignacio also knew only a few feet past where the chest sat was a great chasm, a falling out of the sea floor. He'd been here many times because it was hard to access from the roads, with only a small game trail leading from the thick tree line. He was small enough to come here without a problem, and knew Catalina knew the spot, too.

They'd sometimes had secret meetings on this isolated beach, right before they were going to rob someone or plans for a heist.

Ignacio thought it ironic they'd often been here planning a robbery that might get them each a few pesos when incomprehensible wealth was only a few yards away.

He wanted to laugh and cry all at the same time at the irony of it all.

"Why are you smiling, Ignacio?"

He looked up to see Catalina staring at him. Now he saw she looked nervous.

I've been set up, Ignacio thought. *No wonder she was so quick to accept his invitation to meet tonight.*

"I'm just glad I have a real friend like you," Ignacio said.

Catalina looked away.

Ignacio had a small knife in his pocket and he casually took it out when he heard a shuffle behind him on the beach.

He turned, ready to fight.

"Drop the knife," Arturo said, shining a light in Ignacio's eyes.

There were at least six of them, and they were all armed.

"I'm so sorry," Catalina said.

Arturo pointed at the girl. "You've done well. Go home and wait for our next move."

Ignacio wanted to be mad at her, but he shrugged it off. If he'd been in the same position, he knew he would've done the same no matter who it was.

The famous idea that *there was no honor among thieves* came to mind and he smiled.

"Where is the treasure?" Arturo asked.

"I don't know." Ignacio dropped the knife and dramatically fell down on one knee. "I should've never left the hospital. I'm not doing well."

Arturo stepped forward and loomed over his former boss. "Tell me where it is."

"If I knew I would have it already and I'd be long gone." Ignacio fluttered his eyelids, hoping he looked weak and was going to pass out.

A couple of the other boys stepped up and took Arturo a few steps away, where they conferred.

Ignacio knew Arturo hadn't left his crew. He'd simply taken it over.

Leo stepped forward and helped Ignacio to his feet. "We're taking you back to hospital so you don't die. We'll have someone with you at all times, so you don't trick us. Once you're healed you will take us to the treasure."

Ignacio decided to let them take him back. He did need to heal, and also to plan his next move.

"I have no idea where the treasure could be," Ignacio lied.

ABOUT THE AUTHOR

Armand Rosamilia is a New Jersey boy currently living in sunny Florida, where he write when he's not sleeping. He's happily married to a woman who helps his career and is supportive, which is all he ever wanted in life...

He's written over 200 stories that are currently available, including crime thrillers, supernatural thrillers, horror, zombies, contemporary fiction, nonfiction and more. His goal is to write a good story and not worry about genre labels.

He also loves to talk in third person ... because he's really that cool.

ABOUT THE AUTHOR

Born the same week Animal House was released, Tom Duffy has been on Double Secret Probation ever since. ABBA was also on the top 10 music charts, and Andy Gibb was Shadow Dancing at #1. The author has no problem with any of these things.

Printed in Great Britain
by Amazon